Other Books by Tony Jordan

The Train
Flying Blind
Follow Me and Other Stories

All are available online at Amazon, Barnes and Noble, Books-a-Million, and Kindle.

BREAKFAST WITH FAULKNER

Tony Jordan

Spy Hill Publishing

First Edition

This is a work of fiction. Names, characters, organizations, places, events, and
incidents are either the products of the author's imagination or used in a ficti-
tious manner.

Library of Congress Control Number: 2017906545
Spy Hill Publishing, Clinton, TN

ISBN-13: 9780692880937
ISBN-10: 0692880933

Book and cover design by Nathan Armistead
Printed in the United States of America

*For my grandfather
and for Andrew Lytle, Brinley J. Rhys, Charles T. Harrison,
Father William Ralston,
and especially Father Herbert Wentz,
and Father James Brettman,
without whom I would have ended up, God forbid, a lawyer.
My most heartfelt thanks.*

CONTENTS

PREFACE

WILLIAM FAULKNER, SUBJECT OF A score of biographies but almost forgotten among the current generation of American readers, exerted tremendous force on American and world literature for more than four decades. He is hailed as one of America's greatest writers, having received the Nobel Prize for Literature and two Pulitzer Prizes. Biographies of Faulkner range from the cursory to several-hundred-page tomes that parse his works great and small. But even the most detailed of biographies sometimes miss entirely or connect the dots incorrectly regarding the lasting effects of life events both major and trivial that created the context within which Faulkner crafted his writing. Sometimes the life event may have triggered something as simple as a thought or feeling the writer carried but never shared. Sometimes it may have engendered a sense of loss, feeling of guilt, feeling of responsibility, or another emotion that influenced the writer's work. Sometimes the event might have been a minor deception on the writer's part that had major consequences decades later.

Without full context, a good story can still be a good story, but with complete context it may become a great story. A story of Faulkner's life that includes an exploration of the affectations and roles he might have unconsciously adopted rivals the stories of his novels. In fact, Faulkner's own story can very often be found within his novels in a shaded context in which names, places, and events have been changed—but nuances of emotional response have not.

In some places, the novel you are about to read is long on exposition, but since the story unfolds in a time, place, and culture different from that of today, exposition is included to better illuminate the world as it existed then. I should emphasize that the world of then was quite different from the world of now in the way it judged the morals, ethics, and cultural practices of historical figures. To describe that world, I had options that included exposition, footnotes, or complicated dialogue. For this novel, exposition usually seemed the best choice. Details of scene placement, movement, innuendo, and especially the tone and tint of the words were also important. If a person is crossing his legs, does that mean he is getting comfortable or protecting himself? As with everything, interpretation depends on the situation and the character.

In *Requiem for a Nun*, Faulkner experimented with a part-novel, part-play format. Similarly, some of the narrative paragraphs within this novel may read like stage directions for actors. You may sometimes be wrapped in a scene mentally, as in a novel in which one can be privy to the thoughts of the character. In other cases, you may see the scene from the outside, as when attending a play. I think these juxtapositions work, however you will make the final determination.

But this novel is about much more than William Faulkner. It's about a time, a place, and a people. Faulkner is only the occasional winding of the spring that powers the connected cogs that eventually move the cultural clock's hands forward—even if that clock is fifty or a hundred years slow.

PS: When the ku klux klan is referenced in this book, the words will always be in lowercase. This is done with purpose. It is the right and proper way to refer to the "ku klux klownsmen," as the Judge calls them. You'll see.

PROLOGUE

LATE OCTOBER 1938. THE WORLD is in an ever-tightening spiral toward global war. In the United States, isolationism is the watchword. In the rural South, the Great Depression hangs on, although the Rural Electrification Authority, the Public Works Administration, and the Civilian Conservation Corps are enjoying small successes.

Slavery is legally gone. The land is worked by a tiered hierarchy of sharecroppers, share tenants, and cash tenants. More than 75 percent of the Negroes who did not emigrate north are farming someone else's land. So, too, are the many whites who lost or are losing their small farms to the banks or to the larger, wealthier landowners. With the Depression, many of the share and cash tenants have fallen down the ladder to become, once again, sharecroppers.

Anger born of frustration with federal intervention and disrupted cultural practices has been molded into a spirit of resistance against real and imagined injustices. Some pursue "The Cause"—restoration of an imagined society with rigid codes for chivalry and honor. Others pursue power through vigilante terrorism and a perversion of the legal system. Those seeking power, wealth, and status use these and other methods to advance their personal agendas. But most of the people are just trying to live today in hope of a better tomorrow. This is the rural South—or, as it is proclaimed by politicians, "the New South"—after Reconstruction.

In this New South, foxhunting remains one of the most democratic institutions. Even tenant farmers and sharecroppers may have one or two hounds to run in night hunts with the larger packs of the more affluent. During these hunts, it is the tenant farmers who, in a mostly convivial manner, share their illicit corn whiskey and fruit brandies with their landlords. As the damp dawn draws closer, the fire around which the hunters have congregated grows smaller, and tongue-scalding thick, black coffee replaces throat-scalding moonshine.

Mr. William Faulkner, the newly celebrated writer from Oxford, Mississippi, and Hollywood, California, has been invited by a prominent local banker to travel to south-central Mississippi to attend this night's hunt. In turn, the county judge has invited Mr. Faulkner for an after-hunt breakfast.

BREAKFAST
WITH FAULKNER

CHAPTER 1

COLLECTING THE DOGS

A WET CHILL HANGS IN the morning air, although the sun has begun to warm the day. By four o'clock, it will be seventy degrees. The morning's flannel shirts will be stripped, and cotton shirtsleeves will be rolled up above the elbows. Still, in the morning, you are grateful for the flannel and a field coat—especially if you stand in the shade made by the weak, slanting rays of the late-October morning sun or are out in the wind, which moves the treetops steadfastly toward the southeast. And if you are driving the dirt roads in an open Packard Victoria convertible searching for your foxhounds, you have the collar of your field jacket secured just below your ears and your hat pulled down to just above them.

The driver of the Ford flatbed truck accompanying our convertible slows, stops, climbs down, and, holding a long, curved cow's horn to his lips, blows hard. Seen in the half light of dawn and from afar, his silhouette might be that of a Saxon summoning men to defend the village from yet another boatload of Viking raiders. *Wooooooo-oh. Wooooooo-oh.* The sound travels through the damp wet of the late-October, wind-driven mist. A dog answers *Aaaahooo…aaaahooo* and soon breaks the tree line, bounding through the russet-colored broom grass, eager to rejoin his pack mates in the cage aboard the back of the truck. Once more, the driver sounds the horn: *Wooooooo-oh.* A pause, and then again: *Wooooooo-oh.* No answer, so they move down the road a piece, where the ritual is repeated. As each dog breaks cover and lopes across the fields, both the driver of the Packard and the driver of the Ford pay particular attention to its gait. They are concerned, because, at this time of year, there are small branches, cornstalk stubble, and other detritus of the summer upon which a dog, rushing headlong upon a fox's scent, might inadvertently tread and injure an ankle or tear a foot pad. But as the number of recovered hounds grows, the two drivers are heartened. There are no significant limps and no blood. A closer inspection will be made at the farm, but the hunt has not cost them the services of a good dog. The only dog they are concerned with is Gumption, who seems, ever so slightly, to favor his right front paw as he rushes to greet his owner.

More than once during the ritual, the passenger in the convertible politely declines to blow the horn when offered the chance to do so by his driver. He prefers to remain seated, shielded from the wind by the windscreen and rolled-up side window of the Packard. However, he does not refuse, when offered, the pewter flask that the driver carries in the pocket of his field coat, drawing deeply each time on the quickly shrinking reservoir of warmth. It helps keep the damp cold from entering his lungs. Would that it could keep it from his legs, arms, and nose, but alas, it is less effective in that regard. He hunkers down behind the windscreen, wiping at his nose with the back of his hand. To take his hand from the handhold on the door long enough to fetch his handkerchief might spell disaster should he be thrown toward the driver as the big car leaps from rut to rut on the red-dirt road. He must wait for the driver to stop to quickly retrieve the handkerchief, blow his runny nose, and replace the cloth in his pocket preparatory to the next cross-country dash.

On the occasions when his driver slows or stops, the driver talks about the land. He points to stands of pulp pine trees or to large stands of oaks and pecans. Sometimes he recites a history of landownership, especially when passing pasture where cows graze. There's something prideful in the driver's demeanor at times and something disdainful at others. The passenger is trying to sort out which names are the ones used when pride accompanies the descriptions and which are those used when short shrift is given to the owners of particular parcels.

After a while, they reach a hard-surface road. The driver accelerates, much to his passenger's chagrin. The flatbed truck with the dogs has disappeared from view, having never turned onto the paved road.

The road cannot be called a highway; its width is more that of a country lane, but at least it is not rutted. It is, however, populated by other vehicles, mostly pickups and flatbeds, coming and going. The driver seems not to care. He speeds down the center of the lane-and-a-half-wide asphalt, overtaking without slowing and hardly moving to the right when approaching traffic threatens. Rather, a tooting of his horn announces his coming, as though he is the London mail coach and everyone must give way. Remarkably, they do, many pulling to their right and some even off the road. Most of the other drivers courteously acknowledge the man at the wheel of the Packard; some lift their hats, while others give salute-like waves. One driver, however, in a green Chrysler sedan, shakes his fist as the Packard shoots past, narrowly clearing the Chrysler's left door. Our driver ignores him.

Around a flat curve the Packard zooms, holding the road as though mounted on rails. The passenger, however, not well secured, is pressed hard against the door, as the driver never brakes for the sweeping *S* the road makes. Just as the passenger is recovering his balance, the car swings into the gravel drive of a general store with gasoline pumps in the front.

The two men in the Packard convertible get out and try, unsuccessfully, to knock the dust of the morning's red-dirt and gravel roads from their hats and canvas field coats. From a distance, they look an unmatched pair. One, tall and slender; the other, short. If not for the pipe clenched tightly in the smaller man's teeth, they might be man and boy. Both wear khakis, boots, and briar-proof chaps. The shorter man is topped by a gray fedora, the taller by a high-crowned, sweat-stained, rabbit-felt Stetson, which makes the height difference even more pronounced. The shorter man carries a blackthorn cane, which he appears not to need. It seems rather more an affectation of status than a tool of stability. Smoke from the smaller man's straight briar pipe curls upward; then, caught by the wind, is hurried away.

The taller of the two men opens the screen door to the store, holding it for the shorter man, who walks through, still trying to brush the red dust from his canvas field jacket.

The store is twice as long as it is wide, with a glass display counter to the left and rows of shelves to the right. In the left back corner of the store, there is a barrel-shaped woodstove with a fire showing through the front grate. There are three rocking chairs, in one of which sits an older man in khaki trousers and a flannel shirt. He is smoking a nose-warmer pipe and whittling what might be the body for another pipe out of a block of cherry wood. He rises as the two men make their way toward him.

"Morning, Judge." The man acknowledges the taller of the two men. "How are you? How was the hunting?"

"Just fine, Jesse. Just fine. Mr. Faulkner, this is Mr. Jesse Ledbetter, the keeper of this fine establishment. Jesse, this is Mr. William Faulkner from up around Oxford. He's a writer."

The shorter man extends his right hand. "Please, just call me Bill."

Taking his hand, the storekeeper pumps it. "Pleased. Folks hereabouts just call me Jesse, or Ledbetter. Your choice." He sits and motions for the others to join him in front of the stove.

"Jesse, before we sit...I was wondering if my tobacco came in."

"Did indeed, came yesterday." Jesse jumps up, jump being a relative term since Jesse is seventy-seven years old. From under the glass counter he pulls a jewelry box sized cardboard container and opens it to reveal several waxed paper-wrapped pouches of pipe tobacco. On the top of the box is a label that announces: "Ribbon Cut Cured Virginia with Peychauds. For the Honorable Archibald Cameron." The return address is that of a tobacconist in New Orleans.

The Judge takes a pouch, opens it, and offers it round. Jesse declines, but the writer takes the pouch and, pinching a few of the ribbons, stuffs them into the bowl of his pipe. The Judge does the same with his Dublin pipe. He sits in the rocker closest to the stove. Reaching down, he takes a piece of poplar kindling, strips a good size "switch" off of it, and sticks the switch through the grate of the stove. He offers the lit tinder to Faulkner, who takes it and holds it above the bowl of his pipe, sucking on the pipe's stem to create a draw.

Then the Judge, having lit his pipe and enjoyed two or three good puffs, leans back in the rocker. "Hunting was good, Jesse. Ran two foxes to ground. Must have had fifty hounds or so in the pack. Come light, we rounded up all the dogs in under an hour. At least I got all my dogs in under an hour. Fairly near some kind of record. Nobody's hurt, although I did detect just the slightest limp in Gumption as he was coming across a cornfield."

Faulkner, silently drawing on his pipe, extends his feet toward the stove. The heat feels good after a night in the woods and the chilling wind of an open car. After another puff, he offers a critique of the tobacco.

"I think this is one of the most unique pipe tobaccos I've ever tried. It's exceptionally mild, and the flavor is very pleasing. May I ask the recipe?"

The Judge draws on his pipe then replies, "Peychaud's bitters and cane sugar. They start with a cured Virginia tobacco and then soak it in Peychaud's bitters, with just a bit of cane sugar, inside a pressurized container. The bitters and sugar provide a complex taste somewhere between sweet and slightly bitter. The Virginia tobacco gives it a robustness, and the aroma is a little like licorice and orange blossom. I experimented with various flavors until one day I was having a Sazerac at the Roosevelt Hotel in New Orleans. I realized the difference the Peychaud's made, and so I asked the tobacconist to try his flavor-infusion technique with the bitters. And, *voilà!*"

Jesse rocks forward, his pipe wafting a strongly pungent aroma. "It's OK, I reckon, but I'll stick with a good ol' black shag. That stuff is too much like adding Co'Cola to a shot of good whisky."

The Judge draws on his pipe then observes, "Jesse, you would make a good Frenchman. All they smoke are Gitanes and Gauloise cigarettes made from very strong Turkish or Syrian tobacco. Quite honestly, they smell like burning garbage. You go to a club or restaurant, and there's a blue-smoke miasma hanging in the air. The smoke permeates everything, including the food and drink. I like French cuisine well enough, but not when it's infused with the stink of Turkish tobacco."

The Judge stops long enough for another draw on his pipe then continues, "So how's Satchmo?"

Jesse smiles. "He's just fine, Judge."

"How old is he now?" The Judge knows the answer, but he is trying to entice Faulkner into the conversation.

"Going on twenty-five." Jesse looks at Faulkner with a crooked grin that Faulkner can't help but see.

"I suppose this is where I'm to ask who Satchmo is?" Faulkner takes the bait.

"Why, Satchmo is Jesse's pet albino alligator!" The Judge smiles.

"Pet alligator?" Faulkner is intrigued.

"Pet albino alligator. Very rare." The Judge continues, "People come from all over to see Satchmo. Scientists want Jesse to donate him to a zoo, but we figure Jesse sells more goods to people because of Satchmo."

"Yep, caught him down on Jordan Bayou. I was fishing for bass, and next thing I know I've got this two-foot-long alligator on my line. I pull him in, and he's all white. I figured I'd sell him, but then I put him in a pen out behind the store, and people started coming to see him. I reckon I get ten, fifteen visitors a month just to see Satchmo. And they always buy something, so he's good for business."

"And what does he do in the winter?" Faulkner asks.

"Well, pretty much what other alligators do. He kind of hibernates. Doesn't eat as much and is a little sluggish when he does, but he seems to tolerate the moderate winters we have down here. I built a burrow in his pen, and when it gets cold he likes to sleep or hibernate, or whatever it is he does, inside it. Want to see him?" Jesse pushes himself up from the rocker. He walks to the back door of the store.

"See, I put him in the back so people have to go and come through the store. Helps with sales."

Faulkner reluctantly leaves his position near the stove and follows Jesse through the back door. The Judge brings up the rear.

Only ten feet from the door is a large fenced pond area that Faulkner quickly estimates is about sixty by fifty feet. There is a berm around the pond with large, African-like grasses here and there. It looks a lot like what you might see as an alligator habitat in a zoo. There is a five-foot-high wire-mesh fence surrounding the pond and berm. Jesse touches it and says, "'Course, alligators can't jump, but early on I had some people leaping over the shorter fence I had, just to get inside with Satchmo. Don't understand people. Just because he's white don't mean he won't eat you."

Faulkner peers through the fence at the white snout and dark eyes he sees protruding from under the water. This is no two-foot alligator, for the snout itself is almost two feet long. As he watches for the gator to move, he notices the Judge and Jesse have moved to another end of the enclosure and are tête-à-tête. His ears take in snippets of the conversation.

"They're sure-enough pissed with you this time...don't know where yet...you be careful...those goddamn Gilberts are mean'uns..." All this from Jesse while the Judge nods his head.

A minute or two later, with no movement from Satchmo, the Judge says, "Well, Bill, Miss Julia is expecting us for breakfast. I reckon we should be on our way unless you want to stay and watch Jesse feed Satchmo."

Faulkner declines to watch the gator devour a dead chicken and heads back to the door of the store.

Back in the Packard, the Judge once more speeds along the narrow, paved road before turning onto another rut-filled, red-dirt track. Once again, the red-dust rooster tail follows the car down the road, and afresh Faulkner feels the cold wet seep into his body as the steel-blue convertible jumps from one side of the road to the other as it enters and leaves the grooves and troughs left by logging trucks. Having only just returned from a trip to New York City where winter was just around the corner, Faulkner silently laments the lack of a closed car and wonders why the Judge insists on driving with the top down.

CHAPTER 2

THE HOUSE

THE BIG CONVERTIBLE SPEEDS UP the drive, crunching some of the pea gravel while throwing a stream of the bleached white pebbles backward. The Judge veers left into a circular drive, sliding to a stop in front of the steps of a large, one-story, white house. Built eight feet above the ground, the house has wide stairs leading to an even wider, railless porch that winds its way around three sides of the house. Square, white columns with plain capitals and bases hold up the porch, while the house rests on multiple brick buttresses. Steps and porch are strewn with leaves blown from the oak, hickory, and pecan trees that encircle the house. This morning, the leaves swirl upward in eddies at the corners of the porch or are swept along in long trains as the wind gathers them up. They whisk by rocking chairs in motion, as if ancestors rock themselves, waiting impatiently for All Hallows Eve, which is but a day away.

Bisecting the area under the cedar-shake, hip-roofed, one-story house is a ten-foot-wide stream that serves as a house-cooling mechanism for the hot, humid Mississippi summers.

Prior to the recent electrification, it had also provided the chilling for a cool room, constructed of brick, between the piers on the north end of the house.

Tall windows reach down to the floor and, with the lower sash up, provide access to the twelve-foot-deep porch. Today, those windows are closed against the morning chill and autumn's colorful parade of leaves.

Off to the right, Faulkner can see a large barn some hundred or so yards distant. It is in an excellent state of repair and sports a new coat of red paint. There are other outbuildings that peek in and out of the cedar, oak, hickory and pecan trees that dot the property. Behind the barn he can see some chicken-wire dog pens, and then the land slopes away across an open field to a large pond in the distance. Beyond the pond, Faulkner can just make out the metal roof of a largish one-story building. It looks surprisingly like an aircraft hangar. He thinks this because he can also see a twenty-knot wind sock at almost full extension mounted on the roof of the building. He reminds himself to ask the Judge if he has an airplane.

CHAPTER 3

THE DOGS AND LITTLE ARCH

ARRIVING AT THE FARM SOMETIME in advance of the convertible, the flatbed had continued to a spot behind the barn, the driver backing it up to the dog pens. Squeezing himself from the driver's seat, a young, very large—as in six feet four inches tall and 240 pounds—light-skinned Negro opens the gate to the dog pen and then the hasp on the wire-mesh cage on the back of the flatbed truck. Thirteen foxhounds all try to dismount the truck at once, causing a crush at the narrow opening.

"Heeere now, Gumption! Back up, Sheba! Control yourself! I swear you dogs are positively stupid sometimes. Absalom! Quit biting your brother!"

The young man bravely reaches into the scrum of dogs, grabbing a collar here and the scruff of a neck there, until each of the dogs finds its way into the large, sand-covered pen. Others have prepared the pen for the dogs' return, so troughs of food and water are already in place, and each dog makes for the feeding station with a speed the hunters wished they might have shown last night. So hungry and thirsty are the dogs and so plentiful is the bounty in the troughs that there is no need for fighting, and each animal sates itself.

By the time the young man moves the truck to the front of the barn and returns, the dogs have finished the meat and meal slop in the troughs, and most have finished drinking as well. Two or three still lap at the water barrels, but most are now looking for sunny places to plop. They are, after all, completely fagged from running all night, and the pen on the truck is too small for thirteen dogs to lie down. The young man watches them move about, eyeing them closely for any signs of lameness or soreness. Only Gumption seems to be favoring his right forepaw, and then only slightly. He will come back after breakfast to check them for ticks and to turn them out to run and to relieve themselves in the three-acre fenced dog paddock. He will also make a closer inspection of their foot pads, hoping none have been torn during headlong rushes across rocks, creek beds, and fields of corn stubble.

Since all seems well, Joshua Archibald Weems—known to people in the county as Little Arch—looks at his pocket watch, noting the time. He will enter it in the dog journal and then head home for his breakfast. The watch, a full hunter, looks no bigger than a quarter in his size-fourteen hands. He closes the top and puts the watch back into the pocket of his canvas trousers. He takes good care of the watch. It was a graduation present from Uncle Arch on the afternoon Little Arch walked across the stage over at Tuskegee.

Pushing his gray Stetson high up on his forehead, he opens the dog journal and lays it on the hood of the truck. He enters the time and the notation that no dog save Gumption looks any the worse for wear from the night's hunt. Then, placing the journal on the seat beside him, he starts up the Ford and heads to his house, which is a half mile down the red-dirt road.

CHAPTER 4

WASHING UP

As they leave the car, the Judge reaches back to extract a shotgun from a dash-mounted holder in the front seat. Releasing the pump lock and holding the butt of the stock against his thigh, he pumps the shells into his right hand. Faulkner, still using his hat to knock dust from his jacket, watches and then exclaims, "Good Lord, that thing was loaded! Why on earth would you carry a loaded shotgun in the front seat?"

Pocketing the shells in his field jacket, the Judge replies, "What good would an unloaded shotgun do you?"

The Judge leads his companion around a gravel path to the back of the house, where an enclosed walk of about twenty feet attaches the summer kitchen to the house. At the back of the kitchen is a mudroom.

Hanging up coats and hats, they make efforts to lean over and unlace their hunting boots. While no other efforts of mind or body have given cause for concern this morning, bending over somehow seems no small task. Perhaps this can be attributed to the lingering effects of the previous evening's wet chill and, to some degree, the "antifreeze" they imbibed in an attempt to stave off the stiffening effects of that wet chill. Whatever the cause, neither is quite able to complete the leaning over required to unlace his hunting boots.

Indeed, the corn whiskey has momentarily stranded the writer and his host on the border of the neverland of not drunk but not completely sober—that land of endless possibility, where heroic deeds are doable and every man is either well met or the devil himself. No middle road for the traveler in neverland. All in or all out. It is a land in which many writers, and not a few philosophers, often travel.

Conquering the vertigo of leaning by offering to unlace his guest's boots in exchange for a similar courtesy, Judge Cameron places his right boot on the bench next to Faulkner, who, with not the best of dexterity, manages to unlace it enough for the Judge to draw it off with a bootjack. The Judge returns the favor, and, having managed the boots, both men slip into clogs for the trip to the bathhouse.

Down the outside steps and further down a small draw via a continuation of the covered walk is a tall juniper hedge behind which the original outhouse has resided for a hundred years. An arch through the hedge and a white pergola now lead to a bathhouse where, thanks to the Rural Electrification Authority, there is a hot-water shower, a bathtub, and several wash-up basins. Additionally, there are three commode stalls. Relieving themselves of cups of black coffee, plus other liquids drawn out by that powerful diuretic, the two men soon, with washed faces and combed hair, head back to the house.

Returning first to the mudroom, they exchange their clogs for wool slippers, and the Judge puts on a cotton canvas blazer. Then they enter the at-first pleasing, then somewhat over-warm, kitchen. The Judge is immediately set upon by two bird dogs eager to greet their hunting friend. After a command or two to sit, the dogs do so, but not without quick sniffs of the newcomer's trouser legs. Used to the smell of their foxhound cousins, the two dogs settle down under a large wooden table sporting an ironed, white-linen tablecloth.

There are two place settings at the end of the table, away from the mudroom door. The Judge's wife, arms akimbo, stands waiting, as if for two recalcitrant schoolboys who will, heads down and arms at their sides, shuffle up to admit wrong-doing. Not so for these two, however, is penitence of any sort, for they have returned from the manly pursuit of administer-ing natural justice. In this case, a large number of hounds had been turned loose to find, and run to ground, the fox. Once the fox had taken refuge, the justices of the high court arrived, dug it out, summarily pronounced it guilty of crimes against farmers, and executed it. The blood from the tail was rubbed upon the foreheads of the newest members of the tribunal.

And what, you may ask, had been the crime of this fox? Well, sometimes a fox might make its way past the chicken wire into the coop and escape with a layer or two. But had it been this fox? Perhaps not, but foxes everywhere needed to be aware that such trespasses as chicken stealing would bring swift justice upon at least one of their kind. Of course, no defense was ever offered. No mention of rabbits kept out of gardens, squirrels out of attics, field mice out of grain silos, or snakes who would never threaten a blackberry picker. No, an occasional chicken dinner resulted in perpetual enmity between farmer and fox—and the Judge and Mr. Faulkner had performed their functions as vigilantes of nature, responding to real or imagined crimes; for being foxy was never a good thing, regardless of whether you were in the natural realm or the realm of men.

It is strange that, as given as the Judge and Faulkner could be to hyperbole and poetry, neither of these august men of literature and oral tradition ever addressed the problem of adequate representation for foxes prior to hunts. Perhaps if they had, we might have ended up with *Fox v. Farmer* as a great literary work in addition to *Gideon v. Wainwright* as a great legal one. Oh well, lost chances and lost causes.

Standing now in front of Miss Julia, the Judge, making the smallest of bows, and sweeping his arm underhandedly across in front of his body, proffers, "Mother, may I present Mr. William Faulkner of Oxford. Mr. Faulkner is an author of whom you may have heard me speak. Mr. Faulkner, my wife, Miss Julia."

Miss Julia offers her hand, and Mr. Faulkner, taking it, declares, "My thanks for your gracious hospitality, Mrs. Cameron."

"Please call me Julia. We're pleased to have you, Mr. Faulkner. Arch speaks highly of your work, although I have heard him mutter once or twice about you being difficult to comprehend. Still, he enjoys reading your books, and, Lord knows, these days enjoyment is an oft times difficult thing to find. Now, how is it that such a prominent person as yourself finds his way to the piney woods of southern Mississippi?"

"Well, Miss Julia, I've lived in New Orleans, and I've been up and down the Delta as well as along the Gulf Coast to Biloxi and Pascagoula. I was born and raised in the hills of northern Mississippi, and I've spent time in Memphis and such, but I seldom travel south of Jackson and north of Biloxi, so to speak. When your Mr. Thompson offered me the opportunity to join him for a south Mississippi foxhunt, I thought it the perfect chance to acquaint myself with a part of my home state that so often goes unmentioned in our literature.

"For example, there are one or two places of historical importance I'd like to visit before I go home to Oxford. I would like to drive over to Newton to see the place where the Union colonel Grierson made his famous raid. The people at Vicksburg claim it was the final nail in the local defenders' coffin when Grierson tore up the railroad that was supplying their ammunition and rations. It may well have been as they say, but there were so many other factors it's difficult to tell. And after Van Dorn's raid on Grant's supply train up by Holly Springs had given such hope to the Vicksburg defenders! They thought they had closed the back door when Grant pulled his troops back into Tennessee, but then comes Grierson and does the very same thing to Vicksburg by tearing up the railway and burning the supplies at Newton Station."

Realizing he is probably running on too long, he stops and breathes for a moment then continues, "Anyway, I was very glad of your husband's offer of a hot breakfast after a night of sitting on a log and then tramping through your piney woods in the darkness. And collecting the dogs can be a trial for the cold and tired as well."

"Well," Miss Julia responds, "your host, Mr. Thompson, isn't exactly 'our' Mr. Thompson, but it was nice of him to allow us to offer you breakfast after the hunt. In truth, I was more than a little surprised he would share the company of such a distinguished Mississippian. I only wish he was as sharing with his tenant farmers."

The double entendre of "share" and the subsequent pun on the sharecropper farmers are not lost on the Judge, and while it does not go unnoticed by Faulkner, it causes him only to raise an eyebrow rather than provoke a half smile as it does on the Judge's face.

Motioning Faulkner to a chair, the Judge observes, "Well, if you're interested in Grierson's raid, we can walk down to the meadow where he camped with his cavalry. We still sometimes pick up horseshoes and such."

Faulkner, pulling back his chair, asks, "You mean Grierson camped on your property?"

"Well," the Judge explains, "it wasn't my property then, or even my father's. It was my great-aunt's by marriage. It was five hundred acres her husband had. He was killed at Chickamauga along with my grandfather, and when my father returned to his grandfather's farm in Alabama, it had been taken for taxes by the Reconstruction government; so, he agreed to manage Great-Aunt Belle's farm here in Mississippi. When she died, she left it to him, and he to me. It's a little over two thousand acres now; but yes, Grierson's cavalry camped in the meadow over the hill out back. A day before they made the raid on Newton.

"I notice that you refer to him as the 'Union colonel.' Around here, of course, he's just known as that 'damned Yankee, Grierson.'"

CHAPTER 5

AT TABLE

SCOOTING THEIR LADDER-BACK CHAIRS UP to the table, the first order of business is more black coffee. Then, in order of presentation: a platter of fried, bacon-wrapped dove breasts served with slingshot gravy; a platter of fried eggs; a large bowl of coarse grits; a basket of biscuits; and a plate of thick-sliced cheddar and a softer goat's cheese. Then, small bowls of fig and pear preserves are spooned up from large Ball jars, and some honey, fresh from the hives in the meadow further down the stream, is placed next to a bowl of butter churned just the day before.

Much of the next ten minutes is silence broken only by slurps from the coffee cups and muffled praises for the cooking. Certainly, as each morsel is smelled, chewed, and savored, Mr. Faulkner grins beneath his mustache and mumbles something about ambrosia, nectar, and other such references to food of the gods.

After the fifth or so reference—this one associated with the pear preserves—the Judge stops chewing and, pointing his knife, dripping with cadmium-yellow yolk, at Mr. Faulkner says, "Bill, being a Sewanee man, I can appreciate those ambrosia references—and it is high praise indeed. But you know, around here, you might want to choose your metaphors with a little more care. Folks hereabouts are mostly Baptist, and even the most educated of them have this thing about 'the only God is Jesus.' Now, the only meal they know for certain Jesus ate was some dry bread and what must have been a watery vinegar of a wine. It's possible he had some fish earlier when he parceled out the food to all those people on the hill, but I'm not quite certain that comparing some of the best biscuits in the county to dried bread and comparing this strong, black, boiled coffee to sour wine would be looked on in the manner you mean it. Though I'm sure Mother knows you're praising her work, these dove breasts are better than anything you can get in Paris, and the biscuits are the best this side of Jackson or, if truth be told, the other side too. You should feel honored because Mother doesn't cook for just anyone."

He looks slyly at his wife, who stands next to the large porcelain-and-iron wood-burning stove, her hands in her apron pockets. She winks at him.

He winks back and, laying his fork and knife on the plate, continues, "It's a matter of perspective. Round here the perspective is Jesus is God, and to mention any other god is blasphemy, and yet, your books, if I were to read them aloud to our local residents, would resonate because they are, after all, about Mississippi folks; and human nature being what it is, the locals would identify with the stories and plots. Heck, they might even think they were local gossip, which, by the way, some of the stories might be.

"For example, you know and I know that your books are pretty much stories about your family and other families from the area. We know Colonel Sartoris is your great-granddaddy, and everybody in the South, North, East, or West has some 'Snopes' somewhere in their county. 'Round here, we call 'em Gilberts. Hell, they're the scourge of three counties. Still, the majority of the folks reading your books don't know that your characters are drawn from your real life."

The Judge's use of "hell" draws a glare from his wife, who is refilling the coffee cups from the speckled metal coffeepot. Cursing is something best done in the barn or, on occasion, on the porch when a poacher or horse thief is brought up by the sheriff; but it has no place in her kitchen. She had allowed the earlier "damned Yankee" to pass unremarked only because she did not consider that phrase cursing. It was just descriptive.

Pretending not to notice the scowl from Miss Julia, the Judge continues, "You're a good storyteller, but the difference between you and the other storytellers selling books these days is you make the reader work. It's the difference between hamburger and steak. One or two chews, and down the old gullet goes the hamburger. Tasty enough, especially if there's a lot of fat, but it's gone fast, and you don't ever hear people say, 'Hey, let's discuss that over a good hamburger.' Now, steak… you got to chew on steak. Even a good marbled steak takes some chewing. And when you chew, the juices get all mingled in your mouth, and the meat changes consistency, and when you swallow, you feel as if you've had a really pleasant experience, and you know there's another coming with the next bite.

"Yep, you make your reader work. That's why a lot of people put your books down after a chapter or two. They're expecting a hamburger, and you're serving them a New York Strip—or maybe we should call it a Mississippi Strip.

"Hemingway punches you with words. Steinbeck tells you a descriptive fable like a parent reading to a child. But you, you make the reader participate. You make him look through the eyes of an idiot or a scalawag. You make him synthesize information after you've made him identify with a character in order to obtain that information.

"I like it, but it does take some work. You're not bedside reading, my friend. You're more a rainy-day, cozy-nook, favorite-chair kind of reading. You're 'I'll be damned if I give up on this, because I know when I'm through I will have enjoyed reading it.'"

Through this monologue, Faulkner has continued to butter one of Miss Julia's biscuits and load it with pear preserves. Using his fork, he aligns the pieces of pear so that his biscuit looks not unlike a pear tart being served as a dessert. Then, using his knife and fork, he cuts the oversized biscuit halves into equal pieces and forks one into his mouth. He chews—for the pears retain their crispness—smiles, sips some coffee, savors, and then swallows.

"Guilty as charged," he says. "I couldn't write like Hemingway, too much left out. Details are important. He gives you the actions but expects you to infer the thoughts that lead to those actions. I like to give my readers at least an opportunity to understand why a character behaves as he does.

"I like Hemingway well enough. His books make easy screenplays if you get the right actors. Mine, on the other hand, do not. Even with excellent actors, it's difficult to convey to an audience en masse that which must be conveyed to be understood. Very few directors in Hollywood do internalization or nuance well. There are a few, but they want it to be *their* nuance, not necessarily the writer's."

He takes another wedge of biscuit and, after considering it as it lays on his fork, slowly places it in his mouth.

While Faulkner has been agreeing, the Judge has been feeding the dogs pieces of dove meat and bacon. Eager to intervene but not wanting to cut Mr. Faulkner short, Miss Julia has moved behind her guest and is gesticulating at her husband to cease his actions.

As Faulkner, with the leisure of someone having to be nowhere at any given time, chews his preserves, the Judge says, "Miss Julia is standing behind you sending me all sorts of semaphore messages about feeding Tristan and Iseult some of the dove. I suppose she thinks you'll form an opinion of us as some kind of cracker, backwoods-y types who don't know better and have no manners."

"On the contrary," Mr. Faulkner replies, wiping a bit of preserve juice and melted butter from his chin. "On the contrary. You seem more a sixteenth-century cavalier than a cracker. Tristan and Iseult, are they? And did I hear your man last night call some of your hounds Absalom, Solomon, and Sheba?"

"You did indeed. Far too many Princes and Bugle Anns around. If you're going to teach a dog to answer to its name, it needs to have its own name and not share one with other members of the pack.

"But allow me to gently make one point: you did not hear my 'man' call my dogs. The person who handles my dogs is Joshua Archibald Weems—although his surname should probably be Cameron. He is the great-grandson of one of my grandfather's slaves. At least that's the story we tell. Truth be told, he's the great-grandson of my grandfather, who, after his second wife died in childbirth, found comfort with a comely young house slave named Yaya.

"Joshua has a degree in agriculture from the Tuskegee Institute, and he runs my farm and is a partner in my timber business. He is as much a son to me as my own son, who is currently in Europe studying languages. Normally, Joshua would sit where you're sitting for our after-hunt breakfast. He specifically asked not to attend this morning, though, because he felt his presence might discomfit you. I assured him it would not, but he insisted that until we knew you better, it would be inhospitable to impose our social standards upon you. Personally, I thought his presence would make for a livelier conversation, but we'll have to make do without him this morning—at least at the table."

Faulkner carefully places his knife and fork across his plate and, stroking his chin for a moment, answers. "Well, it *is* a novel concept, certainly in the South. Even in the North you don't see much in the way of mingling of races, especially at meals.

Let's say I might have been surprised, but I'd like to think it wouldn't bother me. Indeed, it would be a new experience—and I'm always up for new experiences. Now, you say he's the great-grandson of your grandfather...but your grandfather's farm was in Alabama, was it not?"

"Astute observation," the Judge notes. "You do listen closely. Yes, it was a ten-thousand-acre plantation on the Black Warrior River, just the other side of the state border. When my father returned from the war, he had been wounded on three occasions; he wasn't up to any heavy work himself. He found his grandfather's former slaves pretty much disenfranchised and living a hand-to-mouth existence, hated by the local residents and exploited by their new overseers. They took him in...cared for him; and, when he was able, he made his way here to his aunt's farm. Twenty-five of those former slave families came with him. Now they all have extended families living hereabouts, and many of them still work this farm as well as their own acres. They form a good part of my constituency in the county.

"Joshua is a particularly bright young man. He and my son grew up together. I tutored them both rather than send them to the local schools. John is considering law school, and Joshua wants to farm, but I suspect they'll both be caught up in this latest insanity in Europe. That's why I have John in Europe learning languages and cultures. When he comes back, he'll be accepting a commission in the army, where I hope they have the good sense to place him in intelligence. Josh manages the farm with me and travels about the adjoining states, buying timber rights in the colored communities. We pretty much have a monopoly on colored-owned timber in the state, primarily because we pay the colored the same price for timber as we do white folks."

Faulkner is listening, but his thousand-yard stare shows his mind is somewhere else. Almost absentmindedly, he says, "Of course, there's always been the concept in the South of the house slave as family, although a lesser kind of family status—such as you might accord to a second cousin you had to take in, or an unmarried aunt left around after your mother or father has died."

Suddenly he catches himself. "Please excuse me. I did not in any manner mean to imply that Mr. Weems is in any way a house slave, but this whole color issue is difficult to discuss without bringing slavery into it...I often find myself explaining potential ideas I could use in novels. Sometimes I talk aloud without realizing it..."

Quick to accept the apology, the Judge urges, "Think nothing of it." He waves the remark away with the fork in his left hand. "Of course, slavery still pervades thought in the South, especially when one considers the future of the Negro. In your books, you never provide any sort of polemic on your views of slavery, but it does not require too much reading between the lines to understand your position—especially in books like *Absalom, Absalom*, which, by the way, I found a disturbing read. Perhaps because it hits too close to home. A great deal of what you have written to date has expressed emotions concerning aspects of life and history that constitute part and parcel of my life and history, thus it can sometimes be a trial to experience your more-than-insightful words.

"You say your initial impression is that I remind you of a cavalier, and I can see why you might think that. The farm, the foxhunting, the fact I am a magistrate…that I have a classical education. Were you to delve deeper, you would discover I speak French, Italian, and a smattering of German. I play the piano and think I can sing. I am the son and grandson of veterans of the Not-So-Civil War, and thus I have certain predilections regarding government and freedom. We can, if you choose, discuss this further in the future, but for now you should understand that I am not an unreconstructed Southerner. Neither am I a reconstructed Southerner. I do not pay lip service to the concepts of honor and duty while fleecing my neighbors of their money or property. I do not wave the battle flag shouting slogans about freedom from tyranny while repressing others because of their skin color or religion. I am a man of tolerance for most things, exceptions being intolerance and the practices thereof.

"I know I shouldn't end sentences with prepositions, but sometimes the situation warrants breaking the rules of grammar and such. Wouldn't you agree?"

The Judge tries to lessen the tension he knows always builds when speaking of Negroes and slavery. He leans his chair back onto its rear legs, catching himself with his knees under the edge of the table. As he does so, he lifts his coffee cup to his lips and, looking at Faulkner over the rim, waits for an answer.

Faulkner—now on his fourth piece of biscuit and pear—swallows and then tries to mirror the Judge's leaning-chair routine, but finds himself unsteady, and, stopping his backward motion with his hands grasping the table edge, returns his chair to four legs on the floor.

"Well," says Faulkner, "I must say, you are much more forthcoming than most people I meet. In some ways, you're like Hemingway. He's right up front—man's man, wounded war veteran and all that goes with it. Like you said earlier, he punches you and sticks out that barrel chest. 'This is me,' he says, 'deal with it.' Yes, he is very straightforward—very. That's why he writes about boxing and bullfighting. Man imposing himself upon man and nature.

"I like to think I belong to the school of the more subtle, more Southern, if you will. Feel your way along. Who are your people? Where did you go to school? Who do you know? The thrusting and parrying of foils as opposed to Hemingway's saber-slashing attacks.

"Then again," he continues, "I suppose, given that our time today is limited, I think you prefer not to play the old get-acquainted game where we feel each other out—trying not to tread on tender toes and all that. Yours is a unique approach that either succeeds famously or fails abysmally. Would you agree with my assessment so far?"

The Judge, landing his chair back on its front legs with a thud, pushes it back from the table. Standing, he takes his cup and saucer in one hand and, with his free hand, motions towards the walkway to the main house.

"If you'd like to be more comfortable, I suggest we go to my office."

He moves off but comes back quickly. Leaning over the shoulder of his wife, who stands at the stove stirring salt pork into some simmering green beans, he kisses her on the nape of her neck and whispers into her ear. "Like he said, nectar of the gods. As far as ambrosia is concerned though, too bad he couldn't have had some of your orange, coconut, and pecan ambrosia. But then, I guess we'd never get him away from the table."

CHAPTER 6

A More Serious
Discussion Awaits

THE JUDGE TURNS, DRAINS HIS cup, and places it and the saucer on the table. He leads the author out the door, along the enclosed walkway, and into the center hall of the main house. Faulkner notes the walkway is ramped up to the house and there are no stairs to climb—though the ramp itself is fairly steep. It is covered in coconut-husk matting, tightly tacked down so it does not slide.

The hallway bisects the house from front to back. At its midpoint, another hallway bisects the house lengthwise. Each hallway is about ten feet wide and is furnished with an eclectic choice of what appear to be mostly Federal- or Queen Anne–period tables and occasional chairs made not of cherry or maple but of what appear to be local woods, with some mahogany here and there. The floors are twelve-inch polished pine boards. Strategically located along the edges of the hall floor are vents that Faulkner knows provide access, when opened, to the cooler air under the house. The cathedral ceilings extend upward to at least fifteen feet, coming to a flattened apex under the hip roof. In that apex are other vents that can be opened under the roof to allow for heat to vent upward. Ropes run through decorative grommets down the walls to open and close the vents. Each end of the hallway has tall doors that, when opened, provide cross ventilation. The walls are plastered and painted a bright yellow with white wainscoting and moldings. The ceiling is painted white and looks to be made of cypress boards. On the walls, every ten feet or so, are mirrored sconces that hold small oil lamps. Apparently, although the house has electricity, its entirety has not yet been wired.

Rather than opening inward or outward into the hallways, it appears all the internal doors are pocket doors that slide from left to right. Seeing Faulkner looking at the doors, the Judge explains, "Keeps them from interfering with the airflow along the hallway."

Proceeding toward the front and turning left where the hallways cross, Faulkner is led to the second door on the right. The door opens into a room at one of the front corners of the house. The room is large and has two tall windows opening onto the front porch and two more onto the side porch. The ceiling is at least twelve feet, maybe more. The room is a Confederate gray on three walls, while the wall to the right of the doorway is hunter green. Midway in that wall is a fireplace with a white, wooden surround and mantle. Above the fireplace is a large painting.

CHAPTER 7

THE PAINTING

IN THE CENTER OF THE painting, a DH-4 bomber flies onward while action swirls around it. Off to the top right, a Sopwith Camel chases a German Albatross, while some distance below the DH-4, a Neuport spirals out of control, - smoke trailing from its engine. Other, more distant dogfights are taking place all over the large canvas, but the DH-4 motors on.

It is an impressive piece of war art, and Faulkner wonders to himself whether it is related in some manner to the Howard Hughes movie *Hell's Angels* or maybe, he thinks, to the movie remake of *The Dawn Patrol* that will be coming out in a few months. They have Errol Flynn starring in this one. Not much in the way of script writing needed, because John Monk Saunders, having written the story from which both the original movie and the remake are adapted, is doing it.

Faulkner stands looking at the painting, transfixed by the gray-white and blue sky. He is mesmerized by the brilliant reds and blues of the Allied aircraft roundels and the stark black-and-white crosses on the German Albatrosses. He stands stock-still while his eyes flick from the DH-4 in the center to the individual dogfights swirling around it.

The painting has caught him off guard, and thoughts are suddenly diving through his mind like the Albatross in the corner of the painting. This is what he had missed. This is his Achilles' heel. He is never going to be a man of action. His moment eluded him, just as it eluded John Monk Saunders, who—although he actually became a pilot in the Air Service— never made it to France. The story Saunders tells in "The Flight Commander" is someone else's, not his. Such was also the case in Faulkner's own "Dead Pilots" and The Ace."

It simply is not fair, he thinks. Not fair. Still, the knowledge is his secret. As far as the world is concerned, he joined the Canadian branch of the Royal Flying Corps and became a pilot. He has the photos of himself in an RFC uniform, replete with wings, to prove it. Yet deep within his mind, somewhere behind the ably contrived and well-told memories, somewhere on the edge of conscious thought, hangs a cloud. A cloud composed of doubt, fear, guilt, and regret. A cloud he had believed blown away, until three years ago when his youngest brother died, flying the airplane that he himself had sold him. At this moment the cloud has become larger, darker, and more threatening.

The Judge breaks the spell. "Captures your eye, does it?"

"Yes, very much so," Faulkner replies. "Are you an aficionado of aviation art?"

"Not particularly," says the Judge. "That was a gift from some friends in London. It's supposed to be my aircraft, and, in fact, it does have the right markings, but I suspect the artist has a production line with a space in the middle that says 'insert client's aircraft.' Still, it reminds me every morning that today and tomorrow, ad infinitum, are all gravy."

"How's that?" asks Faulkner. "All gravy?"

"You know," says the Judge. "You don't put the gravy on the plate until the meat has been served. It's all gravy now. It's just a way of saying that war was pretty much flying into hell, and if you survived that, then whatever life throws at you later is…what was that other expression the Brits were fond of? Of course—'a piece of cake.'"

"That's your aircraft?" Faulkner asks, somewhat incredulously. "You were a pilot in the war?"

"Actually, I was one of the oldest pilots in the war. After Sewanee, I kicked around Europe doing odd jobs like teaching English and being a tour guide for Americans in Europe. I was learning some languages myself, much as my son is doing now. When I came back to the States, there wasn't much in the way of things happening. My father still ran the farm, so I applied for a commission in the Army Signal Corps. It was a good way, I thought, to get some free training in engineering, telegraphy, surveying, and such.

"Well, after a year of tramping uphill and down, I saw this notice requesting volunteers to be trained in flying. That was in 1914, before the war had started. Well, they told me I was a bit old, but I took the physical tests and, having been an athlete and hunter most of my life, ended up passing and getting trained to fly. By 1917, I had more time in the air than most of our pilots, so I was sent to Dayton, Ohio, to test the conversion of the DeHavilland DH-4 from the Rolls Royce engine to the Liberty engine. By the time we entered the war, I had considerable flying time in the DH-4 and ended up flying it in France. When the war was over, I decided I had had enough of the army for a lifetime and came home to the farm."

CHAPTER 8

En Garde

"After the war, a few medals and four working limbs still couldn't get you a decent job, so I decided to dabble in politics and managed to get myself elected magistrate. I've been one ever since. Being a magistrate isn't always a full-time job, so I have time for the farm and the timber business...and we make enough brandy to supply a few places down on the Gulf Coast and in New Orleans.

"We take great pains not to sell or supply anyone in our still-backward state, but there are a lot of places in Louisiana that will buy our small production. Everybody worries about bootleggers because they make 'shine. The authorities keep looking for people buying corn and sugar and such—and we just pick peaches and pears and apples. We also produce some apple and pear vinegars, which we do sell locally, mostly to people putting up fruit and pickles. But our brandies, which we fly out of the state labeled as vinegar, are top-notch.

"Speaking of which, I know it's early, but would you care for a sip? We have a peach and a mixed pear-and-apple orchard down the hill aways, and this is as good an eau-de-vie as you'll get anywhere—including France or in the Caucauses. We triple-distill it, but what really makes it good is that we age it in small casks made from peachwood. The casks are made for us by a local cabinetmaker. We mostly use wood from our own orchards, but I have been known to buy some older peach trees from some of my neighbors, and last year, I heard about a place over in southwest Georgia that was taking out a peach orchard to put in peanuts, so I offered to cut and stump it for a lot less than they would have otherwise spent. So, we have a stock of peachwood curing in an old smokehouse out behind the barn. We reuse the casks, and that makes a big difference as well. In fact, it really isn't a true eau-de-vie because the peachwood imbues it with a pleasant, light-amber color you almost might say was 'peachy.' We make a pear brandy as well, but my favorite is the peach."

Faulkner seems just a little overwhelmed by all this information. The Judge crosses the large room, going behind a desk that fits the room to some closed cupboards in the corner. He opens a door of the left-hand cupboard revealing an assortment of glasses and decanters on silver trays. From one tray, he lifts a large, bottle-like decanter with a glass stopper. Holding it up so the light from the window passes through, the Judge ensures that Faulkner can see the amber liquid. It looks like liquefied gold. Taking the stopper out, the Judge pours munificent portions into two brandy snifters. Replacing the decanter, he returns and offers one of the snifters to Faulkner.

Then, as if from nowhere, the Judge says, "Never use leaded crystal decanters. They look pretty, but I'm convinced they change the taste of whatever it is you've stored in them. Might be from the corrosive effect of the alcohol on the lead in the glass, but, over the years, I've discovered plain glass is much better."

Arrayed in a semicircle facing the fireplace are two large, leather club chairs flanking a matching three-cushion sofa. Placed between each chair and the sofa are four-legged tavern tables made from a wood that looks not unlike the amber liquid the Judge holds in his hand. As the Judge moves to one of the chairs and motions Faulkner into the other, the writer asks, "Peachwood?"

"No, pecan," says the Judge. "Several years ago, a storm uprooted three of our pecan trees, so we cut them up and had some furniture made. Looks a little like hickory crossed with cherry with just a natural oil finish. I prefer local wood, but we do have a few mahogany pieces. My daddy got the mahogany in trade for some of our brandy. It came up from Central America to New Orleans. Our cask maker also does furniture, so most of what you see is his handiwork, or his father's before him. Mahogany is all right, but I prefer the pecan, hickory, and walnut. The desk, for example, is walnut from a tree on the property. There's a lot of yellow pine in the drawers and such, and, of course, the floors throughout the house are all yellow-pine heartwood that was grown on the farm."

Having warmed the brandy glass in his hands, the Judge offers it up in an unspoken toast and takes a sip. Faulkner responds to the toast with a nod. Placing the glass under his nose, he smells the liquid, swirls it, and smells it again. Only then does he sip the amber fluid.

"Amazing! Absolutely amazing! This tastes as good as any brandy or cognac I've ever had."

Nodding in response, the Judge—elbows on the chair's leather arms, glass held lightly in two hands just below his nose, and a slight smile creasing his eyes—replies, "I must say, you are a most agreeable guest, but you may be venturing a mite too far with your superlatives, what with the dove breasts and the pear preserves. Still, nonetheless, we thank you.

"Now, a word to the wise. What you are drinking is a product of our farm, and we refer to it as fruit vinegar. As you know, our state does not allow production or sale of alcoholic beverages, so we distill vinegar from the fruit we grow."

The Judge winks, and once again his guest raises his glass. This time Faulkner takes another, larger sip—confirming the Judge's assessment of the previous evening that Mr. Faulkner's rumored predilection for alcohol is probably grounded in fact. Watching Faulkner's eyes closely, the Judge says, "I understand you are a pilot yourself. Royal Flying Corps, wasn't it?"

Faulkner glances quickly upward at the painting above the fireplace before answering. "Yes, I couldn't get in the US Air Service, so I joined the RFC in Toronto. Short career, though. War ended, and I wound up with a twisted knee from an accident." He nodded to the cane propped against the side of the chair.

Then, almost sotto voce, he says, "Haven't been as interested in flying for a few years now." Faulkner almost gulps a slug of the brandy, hugging the glass with both hands.

"Yes, I can understand," replies the Judge. "I read about your brother's accident. They never came to a conclusion about the cause, did they? Those WACO Cabin Cruisers can be difficult to handle at low altitudes."

The Judge treads lightly here, watching Faulkner's eyes all the while, having noted the momentary hesitation when he asked about the RFC. Faulkner's glance at the painting seems to have steadied him only a little, and his desire to move the discussion onward from flying seems unusual given his initial enthusiasm about the painting. Was it the loss in 1935 of his youngest brother, Dean, in the accident, or was it the RFC that he didn't want to deal with? Perhaps both. The Judge watches his guest's movements, looking for body-position and facial clues. After fifteen years as a magistrate, he is a past master at reading people.

Faulkner takes yet another, still larger, gulp, and the Judge asks, "Flying aside, I was thinking we might know a few of the same RFC people. As you might guess, since I was testing British-designed DH-4s, I had lot of contact with RFC types. Some of them shuttled between Dayton, where I was testing, and Toronto, where they were forming up some of the Canadian recruit units."

The Judge does not wish to discomfit his guest unnecessarily, but as he is quite taken with Faulkner's writing, he wants to know more about the man. He has already breached the wall with his earlier pronouncement implying that Faulkner is like a traveling poet who finds subject matter in family histories, much as the traveling bards of the Middle Ages embellished the history of their hosts' families. He wants to know how much of Faulkner himself is in Faulkner's stories.

The writer does not reply to the query of friends in common. Rather, he turns the question into a question. "The painting, then—it's a gift from some of your RFC friends?"

"Yes. We had a London reunion some years back, and several of them surprised me with the painting. That particular mission was a photographic reconnaissance to confirm the damage inflicted by the previous day's bombing missions to cut a variety of bridges in the Sambre area. Confirming the Germans had no way to reinforce the area, the British and French launched a concerted effort and drove a five-mile-deep indentation into the German lines that was almost fifty miles long. It turned out to be the last battle of the war. The Germans agreed to terms a couple of days later."

The Judge stretches his long frame in the chair and looks up at the painting. "Sometimes I sit here and contemplate what it must have been like to be the pilot of that Neuport or one of those Albatrosses going down in flames. Dying in almost the last action of a war. I suppose it's the fate of someone in every war. Such a waste.

"But then, the entire war and its tens of millions of deaths was a waste, wasn't it? And for what purpose? Just look at Mr. Hitler and his crowd. There'll be another war for certain, and whereas we had only machine guns and rudimentary tanks and airplanes in the Great War, for this next one we will have killing machines and explosives that only writers with fantastic minds could have imagined in 1914.

CHAPTER 9

WAR AND LITERATURE

"THERE'S AN H. G. WELLS novel called *The World Set Free*. Have you read it?" asks the Judge.

Faulkner holds his glass higher as though to admire the color of the golden liquid from the bottom. "Yes, of course I've read it. Carolinium, he calls the substance. It never stops killing. But he salvages a new world order from the ashes of the old. Isn't that what the Great War…"

Here, Faulkner motions to the painting above the fireplace. "Isn't that what the Great War was for? The war to end war? Isn't that what Mr. Wilson's League of Nations was supposed to prevent, another war?

"So much of what Wells writes requires war, or the preparation therefore, as a catalyst for action," continues Faulkner. "Did you read his *The Shape of Things to Come*? He published it about five years ago. Same outcome as *The World Set Free*, but instead of the dictator's rise being fostered by overwhelming power found in an unknown substance, it comes out of a war triggered by unemployment. The movie Alexander Korda made gives fairly short shrift to the economic causes. But if Wells was trying to make an analogy to the current situation—well, he missed the boat, what with Mr. Roosevelt's New Deal and Germany's national socialism. Still, Wells will have his war, and whether a new world order will result—or even can result—is a debatable matter."

Faulkner shifts his position in the chair and concludes, "I'm afraid Wells's intellect is beyond mine. His concern is with mankind; mine is just with man—in most cases, one man...or woman. Wells treats men as a collective organism while I approach men not from the collective mentality but as individuals constrained by history, family, ability, and fate."

"Interesting perspective," the Judge says, rising and moving toward the fireplace. Placing his glass on the mantle, the Judge reaches down to the fireplace and lifts a small piece of pine kindling. Extracting a trench lighter from a pocket of his vest, he spins the wheel against the flint and applies the resulting flame to the kindling. Blowing out the lighter, he places the kindling under the split logs. Before he can complete the move of standing, the fire blazes up. Well-seasoned wood and pine kindling make for fast fires. As the Judge finishes standing, he puts out his hand for Faulkner's all-but-empty glass.

"I think we have time for another before I have to get you back to your host."

Faulkner gives over the glass without comment, and the Judge strides across the room to once more charge the snifter. Faulkner continues to contemplate the painting.

Returning, and handing the glass to the writer who remains firmly seated in the club chair, the Judge continues from where he had left off. "It's an interesting perspective, because your writing is being touted by some as an example of a groundbreaking new literature out of the South. You aren't mired in the 'glorious-crusade' or 'lost-cause' topics that have suffused Southern literature these past seventy or so years. Your writing is more realistic and less romantic. It speaks from the raw emotion of human nature. The stream-of-consciousness technique you've started to use is very much different than the unseen narrator that others use. Wolfe used stream of consciousness well in *Look Homeward, Angel*. Still, I understand his initial draft was treble or so what was published, and much of what was published was done by his editor. That fellow from Scribner's—what's his name?"

"You mean Maxwell Perkins?" Faulkner sips at his brandy, now appreciating the smell as it mixes with the aroma of burning pinesap.

"Yes, Perkins," nods the Judge. "I don't know much about editing, but I think I might defend my pride of authorship too ardently to be a decent writer. How do you feel about editors?"

Faulkner, peering at the fire through the flaxen liquid in his glass, thinks for a moment. "No more than necessary evils, I suppose. Many of them, like Perkins, are the portals to publishing. Without them, you never get your work in front of the reader. Any reader other than the editor, that is.

"When you're just starting out, it doesn't pay to stand up to an editor, because he can scuttle your effort and make all your work for naught. On the other hand, once you've had some success, you can begin to agitate for fewer changes if you don't think the changes make your work better.

"For example, I like to write like people talk. People don't use apostrophes when they talk. They say 'aint' and 'caint' and 'dont.' They sometimes slur words together to make sounds that outsiders don't necessarily understand at first. They run thoughts together, and sometimes they don't take a breath where you think they should. It's all part of authenticity. Part and parcel of being in the action as opposed to being an observer. That's what stream of consciousness is about—being part of the scene, not just looking at it as one does a movie or a play. As you so succinctly put it, 'looking through the eyes of the idiot.'

"Good Lord, e. e. cummings doesn't use capitals, grammar, or punctuation—and he's a darling of the poetry people. You'd think they'd let me drop a few apostrophes here and there.

"As for Wolfe, he was one of a kind. I can't believe he died last month. I thought we had TB under control. Like with anyone, you think you have so much time you don't do some things, and then there's no time. I'm sure we would have had some interesting conversations.

"I think he was more the connection between the old Gothic style of writing and the new style. I sometimes wonder if the original manuscript of *Look Homeward, Angel* might not be better than what was published. Not that Perkins isn't a good editor, but simply because when you shorten something that much, it's difficult to retain the context of the author. And context is everything. Without the appropriate context, the reader doesn't understand the actions of the characters.

"Wolfe was a master of autobiographical fiction, and I admit much of what I write is autobiographical—or at least semiautobiographical—because a writer should write what he knows, and I know my family, friends, and certain people I have encountered or heard about. But like Wolfe, I sometimes have to tell people that what they think they see in my novels—especially if they think they see themselves or their relatives—is sheer fantasy on their part. Because although there are some who might be flattered, most would likely take great umbrage.

"Do you like that word, Judge—*umbrage*? It's a word my earlier editors would wonder if I actually understood. Sometimes I think editors believe that if you don't have a PhD in English and aren't a published master of grammar and diction, you can't write. That's another thing you have to worry about with editors—arrogance. They believe they know the readers better than you do, when, in fact, the readers are just listeners. They like a good story, and when you tell a story, you use your voice to carry off a character. And lots of characters don't speak grammatically correct English, or they speak with broad accents and such. Now that's a long exposition on editors, but they are an important part of the process. Maybe someday we'll come up with a way for the writer to reach the reader directly, but until then, we have to put up with editors."

CHAPTER 10

LITTLE ARCH

JUST AS FAULKNER FINISHES HIS exposition, there is a knock at the door.

"Enter," says the Judge. The door opens, and the opening created is filled with Little Arch.

As Little Arch steps across the threshold, Faulkner realizes that if Little Arch were wearing his Stetson hat, it would be knocked off by the top of the doorframe. Good thing we don't wear hats indoors, he thinks.

Little Arch is dressed in a fresh khaki shirt and trousers and wears a sleeveless leather jerkin over his shirt. The jerkin is held closed by a wide leather belt, which carries a large knife on the left side and what looks to be an empty pistol holster on the right. Rather than the wool scuffs the Judge and his guest are wearing, Little Arch sports a pair of large leather moccasins with hard leather soles and heels. Faulkner has heard them called camp shoes.

Little Arch addresses the Judge. "Uncle Arch, all the dogs are fine. Gumption's got a small tear in one of his pads, but he'll be OK. I moved Sheeba to a separate pen. She's coming in heat again. I was thinking we might want to bring in a dog outside the bloodline since most of our dogs are brothers and sisters and we don't want the problems associated with inbreeding."

He turns to the writer. "Mr. Faulkner, I hope you enjoyed your breakfast. The only cook hereabouts better than Miss Julia is my mama."

"Brave words indeed, Joshua." The Judge looks amused. "Were I you, I'd be careful that my next meal isn't laced with nightshade from Miss Julia's flower garden."

He and Little Arch enjoy what is obviously a private joke revolving around the concept of a flower garden on a working farm.

"Sit," the Judge commands. He does not offer Little Arch brandy, for he knows it will be refused. Later that afternoon, Little Arch will be piloting the Stinson Reliant to the airport in New Orleans to have its engine overhauled, and there is a family rule of no alcohol within six hours of flying.

Little Arch plunks himself onto the leather sofa, crossing his left leg over his right. The large sofa looks like a child's chair with his prodigious frame settled upon it.

The Judge offers, "Our guest and I are discussing writing, airplanes, words, and such. You've read all his books; what questions do you have for our Mr. Faulkner?"

Obviously having considered the possibility of this opportunity beforehand, Little Arch responds quickly. "Well, let's see…You inject a sense of realism-in-the-now into your characters, but you seem not to look to the future; rather, you keep your characters in the present and affected by the past. What about the future?"

"Oh, my," is all Faulkner can muster.

Little Arch stretches his legs toward the fireplace as he shifts at the end of the couch. Doing so, he almost kicks the fast-forming embers of the pine kindling. He catches himself, his feet just short of the andiron.

"Let me explain," Little Arch continues. "Your characters face reality, each in his or her own way. Even when they don't want to face reality, you contrive some event, person, thought, or other device to affect what might be termed a "demi-denouement"—at least in character development. Still, you seldom take your characters' thoughts, actions, or desires into the future. Your novels and your stories just end. Some are open ended, but still they imply no necessary future beyond the moment of time in which they end. What, then, do you think the future holds? Should your characters and your readers be hopeful?"

There is little doubt that this is not what Faulkner had expected from Little Arch. He buys time by swirling the brandy in his glass, once again holding it up to catch the light of the fire. For some reason, now, the dappled sunlight through the four large windows makes the fire seem less powerful. Finally settling on his answer, he begins to speak, but he does so into the fireplace and does not turn to face Little Arch.

"As I was explaining to the Judge earlier, I'm not a futurist. My concern isn't with mankind as a species but as individual men and women. We are who we are, and part of that is what came before us—whether it's ancestry, local history, or the courses of nations. I'm a storyteller. You can put as much of the philosophical or psychological hoodoo in them as you like, but my novels are stories about people in a place and at a time—nothing more, nothing less. If they convey a message, it's because the message was already there. I observe human nature and humans, and if I see a story, I try to tell it in the most complete way I know how to. It's how my mind works."

Little Arch considers Faulkner's reply. "But I'm concerned that while you tell good stories in a unique way, what the South needs isn't just another storyteller, but someone who will tell stories that are hopeful in nature. Stories that, when the reader completes them...well, he feels better than when he started them. Good Lord, if I want to feel sad or angry, I just go into town and take a seat on a bench somewhere north of the railroad tracks. I know all about being doomed by history; I'm a colored man in a white man's world. Don't you have some stories that will make people feel good? Feel at least a little hopeful?

"Consider that when someone plays solitaire with a deck of cards, before every deal there is a hope of victory. And when you play, your chances of winning are increased by how observant of opportunity you are. No matter how many times you lose, the next deal could be the one. Couldn't you craft at least that much hope into your work? Isn't the New South supposed to be about hope?"

Little Arch's voice is a deep baritone, and his passionate plea echoes through the room, having substance in resonance even after the words have ceased.

Faulkner once again considers his brandy before attempting an answer. When he does answer, he offers his response as a question in his thin, quiet, but definitely Mississippian voice.

"Well, just how hopeful do you feel? You say you are a colored man in a white man's world. Does that make you hopeful? The Judge already has us at war in Europe. Does that sound hopeful? Of what hope would you have me write? For example, what do you think the future holds for the colored man in this country? What hope does he have?"

Having successfully avoided Little Arch's question by turning it back on him, Faulkner settles back and sips at his brandy. The Judge, having returned to his chair, remains silent.

Little Arch slowly pushes himself up, his hands leaving large impressions in the padded arms of the sofa. Slowly, he begins to pace in front of the others. His head down, he makes a sweep to the right of the fireplace, reverses himself to the left, and then returns to the middle. Of course, the entire journey is only a total of six steps for the young giant. He stops in front of Faulkner's chair. The light from the fireplace casts Little Arch's shadow upon the writer such that Faulkner feels a chill as the warmth of the fire is broken.

"Our time this morning is short, and there is so much… still…" Little Arch holds his hands in front of himself, much as a supplicant does. "Whenever someone asks me about the future of the colored man, I think of Shylock's speech: 'If you prick us, do we not bleed? If you tickle us, do we not laugh?' That's what everyone quotes. From that, most people interpret the speech as a plea for equal treatment, and are often heard quoting it when discussing equality. Most do not remember the rest of his speech, and if they do, they almost certainly do not use it in an attempt to sway opinion to their side. Shylock's initial words are, in fact, but a prelude to his later references to the cruelty that is unique to those who use 'just' laws to inflict injustice—a cruelty I fear may become the fate of the races in this country.

"I say this because Shylock's speech concludes by demanding equality but, specifically, equality in the righting of a wrong. Then he promises that as the Jews have learned from the Gentiles in what manner such injustices must be handled, they, the Jews, will better even their teachers in the righting of such wrongs. In this case, Shylock promises a cruel outcome beyond even that meted out to a Jew who wrongs a Gentile. So, then one asks, will the Negro, like Shylock, have learned too well from his former masters? Will he attempt to best them in the demand and prosecution of justice?

"Shakespeare does no one justice in *The Merchant of Venice*, for he allows history to prevail, and once again, the Jew is thwarted by cleverness. This cleverness is conceived and carried out by women, and that is the celebration of the entire play. The Jew is bested not just by a Gentile, but by a Gentile woman. In the sixteenth century, this was ignominy upon contempt.

"You, Mr. Faulkner, read this play from the perspective of Antonio. I, on the other hand, read it through the eyes of Shylock, as would any person of color or anyone segregated for his religious beliefs. It may have been a comedy to those for whom it was originally performed, albeit a comedy at the expense of those who are different. But for history, it has become a tragedy. In a manner of speaking, it provided cultural approval for the pogroms of Russia and today's vilification of German Jews. My visit to Germany two years ago and John's latest letters from Berlin suggest the Jew is once again cast as the villain in a very real tragedy. Only this time, the script is being written by a group of psychopaths. And just as Shakespeare induced his audience first to fear and then to laugh at the Jew, so too have today's gray- and black-costumed Punchinellos. Shylock miscalculates when he decides to rely on the Gentile law, and he is then betrayed by that law and those who purport to uphold it. The Jews in Germany have made the same mistake. Is then the Negro to rely on the law for protection?

"I'm not sure what is worse—those who openly hate us and would make laws accordingly, or those who claim to love us as children and would make laws enabling others to speak on our behalf. At least those who hate us do so in equal share as they hate Catholics, Jews, and foreigners alike. Those who treat us as children may be the more dangerous, for they would always have us be children, and they would always want to make our decisions for us.

"I sometimes think the war the Judge already has us fighting may become the turning point for racial equality, but then—like you, Mr. Faulkner—I remember history, and I know that regardless of how well the colored man comports himself in that war, he will gain no respect. Men of color have fought in all this country's wars, and after each, we have achieved no more respect than we had before. Roosevelt's Rough Riders are remembered for San Juan Hill, but in fact, without the all-black 10th Cavalry 'buffalo soldiers' the outcome of that battle would have likely been very different. And in the last war—strange how we call it the last war when all we mean now is the most recent war—American Negro regiments were integrated into French divisions and fought with the greatest of distinction, never being overrun. In fact, the Germans referred to the Harlem regiment as the Hellfighters because of their toughness. Now, when your enemy provides you a sobriquet of distinction, you know you are good. But it was all to no avail. Today, after bleeding in, dying in, and returning maimed from all of America's wars, we have made little progress since emancipation."

Little Arch drops his hands to his side, lowers his head, and, looking directly down at Faulkner, concludes, "Truth be told, a Negro's life is worth less today than it was in 1860. At least as slaves we had monetary value to our masters and could expect to be protected because of that. But now...well, those dogs we ran last night have more value than a Negro. Why, around here if a man steals your purebred Walker hound, not even Uncle Arch is going to find you guilty if you beat that man to within an inch of his life. And if you kill him, well, you'll probably get off with a manslaughter charge and a suspended sentence. In these parts, stealing a man's dog is worse than stealing his wife.

"So, no, Mr. Faulkner, at this moment in time, I don't see much of a future for the Negro in America—but that doesn't mean I can't hope for a better future. It also doesn't mean that I have to accept the status quo. But if I have hope and work for a better future, then I need affirmation that others share my hope and will work in their own way to achieve equality."

Little Arch moves from in front of the writer to the side of the fireplace. Faulkner feels as if a cloud has moved off, revealing the sun. Once again, the light and warmth of the fire reach out and envelop him. He thinks there might be an appropriate metaphor here, but before he can formalize his thoughts, Little Arch continues. "To discuss real change in the future, we should have a serious chat about how, at our core, we Negroes do not share the values of the white man. We are not of the Western canon of philosophy, literature, and government. Historically, our societies are more matriarchal in nature, and we don't share the ideas of Plato, Aristotle, Locke, Hobbes, Rousseau, or Kant. We're treated as if we are some monolithic ethnic group when, in fact, we come from many backgrounds and different places in Africa and the Caribbean. We have no common language, religion, or tradition. So, do we become white Europeans with dark skin, learning their language and values and completely suppressing our ethnic heritage? How do we do that? There are many things needed, but first, we Negroes, in all our diversity, want equal opportunity to express ourselves and to achieve.

"But right now, at this moment in time, if a Negro wants equal protection under law, then he had better move to this county, because it's one of the few places in America he can expect that to happen."

If human ears can actually prick up, like those of a border collie, then Faulkner's do. "Why?" he asks the massive presence to his right front. "Why this county?"

"Because of Uncle Arch. I bet he didn't tell you that he's in the banking business? That he underwrites the majority of poor white and colored landowners in this county and some of the surrounding counties? That this farm's timber, cattle, egg, and pork profits go into financing other farmers and a colored school? That the bank owners and the big landowners—like Mr. Thompson—don't like Uncle Arch much because he keeps them from buying out the small-farm owners and adding those farms to their various sharecropper inventories?

"You should have him tell you about the small farmers' association he formed. It has an equipment pool from which farmers can rent equipment when they need it. It reduces costs considerably. The association also coordinates a group of workers who move between the farms and are paid through the association. That way, farmers don't have to support laborers when they don't need them, and the association can use a smaller group of dependable and proven laborers to support more farms. This isn't a popular undertaking with many of the large-farm owners, because the wages paid by the association are substantially higher than those they pay. This attracts the best laborers from several counties to the association payroll, and subsequently, small, association-affiliated farms produce more per acre in crops and have better chicken and pork production rates than the larger farms."

Here, Little Arch stops. He suddenly realizes that he has become more physical in his speech and gestures. He moves back to the front of the fireplace and looms over Faulkner, much as a black oak might threaten a cabin in a strong wind. In a somewhat sheepish manner, he looks first at the Judge and then at Faulkner. His voice drops the octave it had climbed during his soliloquy. "My apologies for rambling on so. I do so get wound up when talking about the things the Judge is doing." He sits.

Faulkner turns to the Judge, whose face carries a wry smile. "I must say I had no idea about the depth or breadth of your activities. I withdraw my earlier characterization of you as a cavalier. You sound much more like a commissar responsible for a commune. Is that how you see your New South, as a communist enterprise?"

The Judge faces Faulkner, looking across Little Arch, who tries, without success, to sink his body deeper into the leather sofa.

"Communalism isn't necessarily communism," the Judge answers, his baritone voice resonating through the room. "In communism, all property is owned by the state. Here, we are very much about private property and the preservation thereof. But we have come to understand that to resist the transfer of land into large trusts held by the richest, there are certain cooperative actions necessary on the part of the small landowners. What the association practices might better be called cooperativism than communalism.

"Cooperatives are nothing new in agriculture. They have existed for some time. The association just extends it to include laborers. You don't have to be a landowner to belong to the association, and thus laborers can earn additional monies based on their purchase of shares in the association. Think of this cooperative as a savings and loan association. Like the old adage says, there's both safety and strength in numbers. There are more small landowners than there are big landowners, and with a labor force that is well paid, they constitute a voting bloc large enough to mold elections, at least in the county. And so, they are the majority of my constituency.

"Personally, I don't cling to an imagined past where all white Southern men were cavaliers and all the women were ladies in crinoline hoop skirts. I know that concept isn't true, but try telling the truth to those who nursed on mystical milk from the teats of women wailing about the degradations heaped upon the poor white Southerner by the Yankees, Negroes, Jews, and Catholics.

"In truth, life here, just like everywhere else, has always been about survival of the fittest. The strongest—whether economically, mentally, physically, or a combination thereof—get to make the rules. Want to know who the strong are? Go to any county seat on a Saturday. Find yourself a bench near the courthouse and watch. The rule makers wear khaki pants and Wellington boots. Their hats may have sweat stains, but they are not full of holes. They wear leather belts and mostly tucked-in khaki shirts, but a few will wear the occasional summer suit of linen or cotton. People call them 'Sir' and 'Mister.'

"On the other side—the side that doesn't get to make the rules—you'll see overalls, lace-up work boots, and sweat-stained hats with tears in them. Down beyond the railroad track in Negro town, you'll find the same overalls and work boots; the same barbed-wire-torn, sweat-stained hats; and the same tired, overwhelmed men waiting on the same life-weary women to finish their shopping. It has always been so. They live in fear—fear of losing their farms to the bank or to one of the big landowners, fear of losing family members to illness or accident, and fear that the rains won't come, or if they do, they'll bring hail and high winds. Some of them even have to fear for their lives. They believe in Jesus but don't understand how he could allow the suffering they see. They hope for a better life for their children, but don't see how it could happen. And most of all, they believe in the hereafter, where they are promised an existence free from fear.

"You ask if cooperation is our New South, but the New South is no different from the Old South. There are those who make the rules and those who don't. I'm in between the two. It is my duty to see to it that the rules are kept but also that rules are not used to take away individual freedoms or property. Rules are necessary, but common sense is better, and that's what I try to use—common sense. But there are always those who would prefer that I not do what I do, and, mostly, that I would not do it how I do it. They don't like small landowners having any power, and they constantly challenge our association financially and in the courts. Their lawyers attempt to legally intimidate, and their hired thugs threaten physical harm.

You might, when you meet them, think them nice. They may have manners, but like their ilk throughout history, they are not to be trusted. They even threaten me. So, I go about armed and do not conceal the fact.

"We have made progress in our attempt to have real democracy, but I fear all will be for naught when Roosevelt takes us to war. For, make no mistake, the world is in crisis, and unless someone disposes of several Nazis in Europe and the Japanese in the Pacific, there will be a war even greater than the last. Our educated young will go away to fight. Our labor pools will be drained, and once again, a federal government will determine our fate. Such a war will be more devastating than any history has had to offer. It will be even more destructive than our own Civil War.

"Just consider the weaponry of the *last* war..."

CHAPTER 11

WAR AGAIN

THE JUDGE SWEEPS HIS LEFT hand up toward the painting, and Faulkner once again contemplates the large scene above the mantle.

Faulkner understands the Judge. He stares hard at the painting, sits up a little in his chair, and, with a slight move of his glass toward the impressive oil, begins, "It's true that in 1918 those machines were the height of our war-making skills. They could kill as many men in one pass as a rifleman could in a career of battles. They often struck without warning, and their weapons were indiscriminate. A bomb cares not whether you are a combatant or a civilian. Now we have aircraft that can carry a ton of bombs. For example, how many bombs did your aircraft carry?"

The Judge thinks for a moment. "Well, let's see...I think it was two 230 pounders or twelve 20 pounders. Certainly we always thought that if we had larger bombs, we could do the same job with fewer aircraft."

"And now," Faulkner continues, "we have 500- and 1,000-pound bombs, and I understand the Germans and the British may be experimenting with even larger ones. The Germans have firebombs made of thermite that keep burning, not unlike Wells's Carolinium.

"Have you read George Steer's *New York Times* account of the German bombing of that Basque village in 1936? Picasso has done a mural depicting the devastation. I saw a photograph of it in the *Paris Herald Tribune* last year. Of course, you can't appreciate a painting from a photograph, especially when the painting is almost twelve feet high and twenty-five feet long. Still, it is a powerful piece. But firebombs that keep burning sound so inhumane. Perhaps Wells will have his war of things to come…" Faulkner's voice trails off.

The Judge rises from his chair and catches up a poker from beside the fireplace. He moves the logs about on the andirons, sending flames and sparks into the chimney and a few popping embers onto the hearth. With his back still to Faulkner, he leans into the fireplace. His voice mixing with the crackle of the pine and hickory, he says, "Yes, Wells will have his war, and it will be with machines that kill thousands without discrimination, machines much deadlier than the DH-4."

He straightens up and turns toward the writer. "I see from your stories you're not unfamiliar with the DH-4. In fact, you put some of your characters into it in "Dead Pilots." I assume you know we called it the 'Flaming Casket' because the fuel tank was mounted between the pilot and the observer and was extremely susceptible to incendiary rounds. I have to say, it was a damned nuisance having that gas tank mounted where it was. Incendiary bullets aside, it made communication with the observer much more difficult. As irony would have it, we put a self-sealing gas tank into a DH-4 on November 12, 1918. Just a tad too late, I'm afraid. That's the kind of thing you need to put in your novels and stories—the irony of life unscripted.

"While I like most of your efforts, I must admit I found "All the Dead Pilots" a trifle melodramatic. Oh, and there was one small factual error. No DH-4s in the night bombing of Mannheim. That was all Handley Page twin-engine jobs. We didn't fly at night unless we got caught out late returning from a mission."

Little Arch rises. "Speaking of flying, I have to check out the airplane we're taking to New Orleans. Mr. Faulkner, once again, please excuse my homily, but I seldom have the opportunity to preach in front of someone who isn't already a member of the choir."

Faulkner rises and offers his hand. "It has been a distinct pleasure meeting you."

As Little Arch leaves, he turns to the Judge. "I'll see your car is full of gas and all the accoutrements are in place."

"Thank you, Joshua," the Judge replies. "Now, Mr. Faulkner, as I was noting, you have a decided talent for describing certain aspects of life. For example, "The Ace" is an excellent piece of observation, but I would have thought that, given your penchant for detail, you might have included the fear of death that pursues us in the cockpit. You seem more concerned with life on the ground than death in the air. You are spot-on with the aftermath of missions, the braggadocio, and the swagger, but where is the throwing up in the latrine before we swagger out to the aircraft? Where are the wet crotches and the snot- and vomit-stained scarves? What about the fear of a second-generation machine falling apart at twenty thousand feet? The fear of burning to death? The decision to jump rather than burn? The freezing fingers, toes, and noses? The… well, you know. You were there. Why not tell the entire story?"

Faulkner is once again staring at the painting. Only when the Judge moves into his direct line of sight does his concentration break.

"That is a good question," Faulkner admits, "and one for which I don't have a ready answer. Still, only someone like yourself notices the omission. Perhaps it is because I want the pilot to retain the nobility of a knight of the air. I want to emphasize the human side but not detract from the courageous. Perhaps I do not want to invade, too far, the privacy of the individual. Writing about what you suggest might distract the reader from the very things I wish to emphasize."

The Judge listens, one hand on the mantelpiece and the other in his jacket pocket. He thinks that Faulkner's excuses ring as a toll from a cracked bell, for there is no knightly behavior from any of his characters while they are on the ground or in the air. Each is beset by self-doubt or self-loathing, jealousy, hate, or some other such emotion exacerbating his already pitiful life. No, the bell sounds cracked.

The aroma of burning pine bathes the room. The heat has once again reached Faulkner's wool-clad feet and moved up his khaki-trousered legs to his chest and face. It brings with it a drowsiness only slightly interrupted when a small carriage clock in the bookcase chimes eleven.

"Is it far to the Thompson farm?" he asks his host.

"About twelve miles," the Judge replies. "If we leave by the half hour, we'll have you there in plenty of time to wash up and change for dinner."

"Then I suppose we should go." Faulkner takes one last, large sip from the glass and places it on the table between the chair and sofa. Rising, he takes his cane in one hand and his pipe in the other and moves toward the door.

"I must say, this has been a most agreeable and educational morning. I had no idea any of this might happen when Mr. Thompson asked if I wanted to come down and go foxhunting."

Laughing, the Judge responds, "Well, even if we don't ride horses and shout 'Tallyho,' foxhunting is a sociable affair—even with just a bunch of dirt farmers." He opens the door and motions for the writer to go through.

"Speaking of horses," Faulkner says, "I didn't notice any in the fields on our way up. You do have horses, don't you?"

"Nope," the Judge responds. "No horses. We have six mules but no horses. Why would we want horses? I learned early in life that horses, boats, and women are money pits. You just keep throwing away money, and what do you really get? I learned later that airplanes are much the same unless you have a real need for them. We do on this farm. We fly our brandy down to the coast. No roadblocks that way. Horses? Nope, no use for them. The mules will drag a tractor out of the mud, and they'll pull a plow over steep, rocky ground better than a tractor. And on the off-hand chance that we do need to ride somewhere, a mule's more sure-footed than a horse. This is a working farm."

By this time, they are back in the kitchen, where Faulkner makes his pleasantries with Miss Julia and acknowledges two Negro ladies who are cutting vegetables by the sink. The Judge takes great care to introduce Miss Winona and Miss Abigail to Faulkner. They are, he says, the best cooks in South Mississippi, except, of course, for Miss Julia.

In the mudroom, Faulkner, not without some little difficulty, laces on his hunting boots. The Judge slips into a pair of chestnut-brown roper's boots, his khaki pants hiding the embroidered shafts. He then reaches down from the pegs a leather belt with a holster that carries a large pistol. He straps it around his waist. Faulkner, not yet comfortable with his host and perhaps too far off in neverland when they first arrived, has not asked the reason for the pistol or, for that matter, the loaded shotgun the Judge took from the car. Now having a little more understanding from the Judge's statement in the office, Faulkner wants to know more. "Is that a Smith & Wesson? Do you feel you really face an imminent danger that requires so large a pistol?"

"Hmm...I see Thompson didn't tell you much about me before you accepted the invitation to breakfast. It's a Colt. As I said earlier, it is just to let certain parties know where I stand. Let's just say it's a symbol of the New South as well as of the Old South."

Leaving the mudroom, Faulkner carries his field jacket over his arm, as the morning sun has climbed higher and with it, the thermometer. He thinks the flannel shirt sufficient, but when he sees the Judge putting his field jacket on, he remembers the wind from the morning's drive and decides his jacket might be a good idea.

When they round the corner of the house, Little Arch is standing beside the car holding the passenger door open. A shotgun, its barrel pointed skyward, is already in place, having been pushed into the receptacle on the dash. As Faulkner moves toward the door, his diminutiveness is emphasized by Little Arch's prodigious presence. It makes Faulkner feel so small; it is like he is a child climbing up into the Packard's passenger seat.

The Judge slides behind the steering wheel, pushes the electric starter button, and shifts into gear. The big convertible crunches its way down the drive and back onto the red clay-and-rock county road. There is no doubt the Judge is a pilot; he drives like one. The big car careens down the center of the road, kicking up a red-dust rooster tail that would entirely conceal it from anyone to its rear. The Judge knows the road and how to enter and exit the very flat curves. Faulkner is thrown from side to side and up and down as the car's suspension meets the rut marks left by heavy farm vehicles after a rain. With all the to-ing and fro-ing and upping and downing, there seems no time for conversation, although Faulkner has one more question he wants to ask. Each time he starts, though, the Judge takes another turn or the suspension throws the writer as much as six inches off his seat. He returns to the leather upholstery, sliding left or right, and has to grasp the door or the dash to keep from winding up on the floorboard or falling into the Judge's lap.

The Judge, however, drives the road almost automatically and, having the steering wheel and gearshift to hang on to, is giving thought to what he has learned about his guest. He knows for sure that Faulkner has never flown as a combatant in a fighter or even a bomber. A combat pilot would anchor his right leg in the space between the car door and the seat. He would hook his left heel under the front-seat edge and grab the door-mounted armrest with his right hand and the leading edge of the seat with his left. But more importantly, he would not be looking inside the car, as Faulkner is doing. Rather, he would look outside and ahead. He would anticipate the car's responses to the changing terrain, for by watching the road he would understand what was about to happen. No, thinks the Judge, Faulkner has never flown in combat or done much in the way of acrobatic flying either.

The twelve miles disappear quickly, and as the Judge slows to turn up the drive to the Thompson house, Faulkner realizes he has been holding his breath almost the entire way. He is physically exhausted, and the effects of the large breakfast, the morning's brandy, and the moonshine whiskey of the night before have begun to seek release from the confines of his stomach. He will be glad to get down from this monster of a road car.

Now that the car is moving at a much more leisurely pace Faulkner asks, between quiet gulps for air, "Judge, these people who would—how did you put it—rather have you not do what you do…Who are they?"

Downshifting to second, the Judge turns his head slightly to fix Faulkner in a steely gaze. "Why, Mr. Faulkner, I thought perhaps you wouldn't need to ask that question. I thought you would have already recognized them. They see themselves as your cavaliers of the New South. They vow to take back that which was never actually theirs. They are, in fact, our Blackshirts and Brownshirts. They serve sundry demagogues whose lust for power is transmitted downward, so that even the lowest of members feel themselves superior to their neighbors. They stage hunts, like our diversion last night, but it isn't foxes they seek. They are the Knights of the Invisible Empire, the protectors of racial purity in our New South."

He stops the car in front of an impressive two-story brick house surrounded by oak and hickory trees. The large porch is decorated with pumpkins and cornstalks, among which red and yellow leaves from the trees have settled as God's finishing touches to the designer's not-quite-complete autumnal tableau. The front door opens, and a somewhat rotund man in his late forties steps out through the screen door onto the porch. His three-piece gray suit announces, "I am not a farmer!" A gold chain traverses his stomach from one vest pocket to another and is festooned with various gold charm-like insignia.

Leaning over behind the windscreen toward the writer, the Judge says, "They are the klan, Mr. Faulkner, and here is your host again, our local klaliff. You'd best get down and go up to the porch and greet him. It's protocol, you know. He can't come down to greet you. Not done. He's too high up in the organization."

Straightening a little, he again fixes Faulkner with his eyes. From under the brim of the Stetson hat, in the midday light, the eyes seem to Faulkner verily what Solomon's eyes must have looked like when he interrogated the two mothers.

Breaking the gaze, the Judge drawls, "Well, I must say, it has been an interesting evening and morning. You are a most pleasant guest. Do come back sometime, Mr. Faulkner."

"Thank you for your hospitality, Judge, and please thank Miss Julia again. Her biscuits are wonderful." Leaning even closer, Faulkner says sotto voce, "I would certainly like to hear more about you and the klan." The writer extends his hand.

Taking his hand firmly, the Judge nods and says, "Yes, I'm sure you would, but that is a tale for which no ending has yet been written."

CHAPTER 12

THE DRIVE HOME

THE JUDGE BARELY ACKNOWLEDGES BANKER Thompson as he makes the circle in front of the house, narrowly missing the bumper of what he assumes is Faulkner's car—a tan, four-door Ford Touring—its dull color contrasted by red-dust splotches from the Mississippi roads. Turning back onto the county road, the Judge pushes the big Packard up to speed and cruises until he reaches his turnoff. He makes the turn and then holds on to the steering wheel as the car jumps from one deep-cut groove to another on the red-dirt road. He remembers the way Faulkner had grabbed at the door-mounted armrest, belying, the Judge thinks, any significant flying experience.

"That explains," the Judge mutters to himself, "the lack of aerial episodes of consequence in Faulkner's writing. While he can observe, internalize, and then write about what happens on the ground, it is difficult for him to report accurately the feelings one has in the open cockpit of a fighting aircraft. His RFC stories and perhaps a great deal of his aviation acumen must then be part of a cultivated affectation. Much like the cane he carries, for certainly he carries it more like a swagger stick than like an orthopedic aid."

The Judge, always willing to consider every possibility, thinks this affectation might be attributed, in part, to a behavior learned from Hollywood, where everybody is somebody else. It reminds him of the line from Gilbert and Sullivan: "If everybody's somebody, then no one's anybody." The Judge is perfectly happy if Faulkner wants to be somebody else, thinking that the writer must have even changed the way he spells his name. All the Falkners the Judge knows in North Mississippi spell their name without the *u*.

Faulkner is, the Judge muses, extremely observant and good at describing what he sees—including feelings. The Judge is sure Faulkner internalizes that which he observes and then writes about—not from a third-person perspective but from a first-person one. Thus, The Ace and Johnny Sartoris are Faulkner's avatars in his artificial world of the fighting man. Faulkner writes not from his brain but from his heart. People who write from the heart are extremely vulnerable to trauma, both real and imagined. Outwardly, Faulkner appears a normal, intelligent individual, but the Judge suspects an inner weakness fueled by depression and, perhaps, further fed by alcohol and, most probably, guilt associated with the death of his youngest brother. It is what the Judge's father would have referred to as "a deep melancholy for something lost." Perhaps Faulkner, the herald of the New South, subconsciously longs for what he thinks of as the Old South. He might obtain success in the future, but the Judge's assessment is that it is doubtful the writer will achieve whatever it is he thinks will make him happy.

The Judge feels for Faulkner much as he sometimes feels when he has to send a farmer of his acquaintance to the county jail. It isn't sadness so much as disappointment. "Still," the Judge considers, "he writes damn well, even if it takes me a week to read one of his books."

CHAPTER 13

BACK HOME

RETURNING TO THE HOUSE, THE Judge enters through the front door and goes directly to his office. He takes a kit from the lower right drawer of his desk and carefully uses a brush to dust powder on Faulkner's brandy glass. There are some clearly identifiable fingerprints. From the same drawer he takes a Kine Exacta 35mm camera. He places the brandy glass between two gooseneck desk lamps and proceeds to focus the camera on the fingerprints. He snaps, turns the glass, refocuses, snaps again, and so on until he is satisfied he has what he needs. He wipes the dark powder from the glass and places it on a tray that will be gathered up later. The glass will be washed along with other dishes from the kitchen.

He will remove the film from the camera later in his darkroom in the barn and develop the negatives. Once he has classified the prints, the negatives will go into his fingerprint file. He has prints on all the local big shots, just in case he needs them. He also has prints from some of the more frequent criminals and from the most dangerous individuals who have come through his courtroom.

"Never know when prints will come in useful," the Judge mutters aloud.

The last time he used fingerprints was when someone broke into his car and cut his leather seats with a large knife. It turned out to be one of the local klansmen, an inveterate poacher who regrettably refused to provide the name of the higher-up who put him up to the task. The fingerprints the Judge obtained had come from a note left in the car promising an escalation of trouble if the Judge did not lay off the klan. The Judge quickly found a matching set in his files, and it didn't take long to break the klansman's alibi. Still, the man never gave up his klan seniors. The Judge had sentenced him to thirty days in lockup, restitution for the cost of repairing the seats, and suspension of his driver's license for a year. Subsequently, the man had been arrested numerous times for driving without a license, and on each occasion, the Judge gave him more jail time.

Done for the moment, he heads to wash up for dinner. He's looking forward to those green beans Miss Julia had simmering with salt pork when he left the house with Faulkner.

CHAPTER 14

Sunday Dinner at the Thompsons'

FAULKNER'S WELCOME ONTO THE THOMPSON porch is effusive. It is too effusive for his taste. He feels as if he is stepping into a story by some other writer that's being screen-tested on a soundstage. His hand and arm are shaken until he feels he must have pumped a gallon of water from a well. Banker Thompson's greeting is too loud, as if he is calling Faulkner in from the field instead of greeting him on the porch.

"Just in time! Just in time!" The banker pumps his arm once more. Faulkner slips his grasp by shifting his field coat from his left to his right arm. For a moment, the coat hangs as if on a laundry line made by the two clasped hands. The banker releases his grip only when the coat threatens to slide to the floor, and it is necessary for Faulkner to grab it with his left hand.

"Come in! You're just in time to clean up for dinner." Banker Thompson still has a loud voice.

Faulkner is shown to his room. His suitcase is on the floor next to the bed. He strips off his hunting clothes, uses water from the pitcher and basin to scrub his face and hands, and then rubs a washcloth over his chest and underarms. He follows that with some lightly scented talcum powder. Now he no longer smells of tobacco, woodsmoke, or—more importantly in a Southern Baptist household—any kind of liquor. He puts on a white cotton shirt, frayed somewhat at the collar and cuffs, pulls on some dark wool trousers, and ties a half Windsor in his dark-blue tie. He tops off his wardrobe with a Donegal tweed sports coat he purchased in Hollywood. The padded shoulders give him more substance, but the pockets have begun to droop from where he continually puts his hands as he walks. He slides his feet into a pair of well-used brown oxfords and bends over to tie the laces. As he does, the lingering effects of the brandy, whiskey, and lack of sleep cause him to feel woozy, and he begins to lose his balance. He grabs at the footboard of the iron bedstead just in time to keep himself from falling to the floor. He straightens up slowly, his face flushed, the blood just beginning to drain back into his body. After a few moments, he makes it to the straight-backed chair in the corner of the small bedroom and sits.

He doesn't know how long he has been sitting when there is a knock at the door and a young female voice announces, "Mr. Faulkner, Poppa says to tell you dinner is ready."

"Thank you, I'm on my way down," he manages.

Still, the laces need to be tied, so he stands, turns, and steps up so his foot is on the chair. He gingerly reaches down while keeping his head upright, feels for the laces, and ties them. He repeats this with the other foot.

He holds the handrail closely while descending the stairs, but by the time he reaches the first floor, he is his old self. He pauses a moment to remember which is the dining room, but that task is handled for him by Banker Thompson, who apparently has been watching for his appearance. Once again, the hand is proffered and taken, but now it is used to tow him across the back of the hallway and into a dining room that would do justice to any Victorian house. The furniture is heavy and dark. It includes a large china cabinet, an enormous sideboard, and a dark mahogany table that could easily seat twelve. Today it is set for six. Already at the table are Mrs. Thompson and the three Thompson daughters: Alice, sixteen; Rebecca, fourteen; and Lindsay, twelve. All have their mother's dark hair and will more than likely grow to assume her well-rounded figure. Already Alice shows signs of developing a rounder face, and her upper arms have begun to spread. They all smile as he pulls out his chair, which is on Mrs. Thompson's right. Each wears the clothes they will wear to church tomorrow morning.

Banker Thompson prays as if he had missed his calling when he went into banking. Faulkner, being an Episcopalian born of Presbyterian stock, is more accustomed to short, to-the-point, "Thanks, God, let's eat" types of graces. But Banker Thompson thanks Jesus for a whole lot more than the food, including the presence at the Thompson table of such a prominent personage as Mr. Faulkner—a man, the banker claims, who can help restore the glory of the South. Having thanked

Jesus, the banker goes on to ask for a number of boons, including good health, good weather, good crops so the farmers can make their bank payments, a return to the gold standard, and God's direct intervention to put outsiders in their place and allow the good people of the state of Mississippi to determine their own fate. It is a powerful prayer. Faulkner thinks the iced tea in the glass in front of him might just taste like water by the time the banker finishes.

Dinner is a pot roast. Pot roast on a Saturday is one way of showing wealth in the depressed economy. Money does not, however, seem to be one of Banker Thompson's problems unless, of course, it is someone else's money. Along with the pot roast, the Thompsons serve mashed potatoes, English peas mixed with carrots, sautéed yellow squash, and yeast rolls. There is a German chocolate cake on the sideboard for dessert.

Once the food is on the plates, Banker Thompson asks Mr. Faulkner about his morning with the Judge. The appellation "Judge," while not exactly dripping with venom, is sounded more like a farmer might speak of a fox or a skunk. The banker's tone carries the message that he will have little to do with the Judge other than in matters required by business or decorum. While perhaps it is not the banker's intention to convey such a message, it is, nonetheless, the message Faulkner infers from the question.

Having gingerly taken up his iced tea to sip the meniscus from the almost overflowing glass, Faulkner speaks after he lowers the glass to the table.

"It was an extremely interesting morning. I'm impressed with all the Judge has accomplished with his farm." Faulkner does not think it appropriate to disclose the other issues he discussed with the Judge, for the Judge's last bit of guidance before departing had put him on his guard. One does not engage in or allow oneself to be dragged into discussions of politics with members of the klan, especially not with members who can voice what appear to be reasoned, if overly passionate, arguments.

"He is also a very well-educated man." Faulkner thinks this might divert the banker. "And a decorated war veteran. Yes, indeed, he is a most interesting man," he adds.

"Yes, although I'm not sure you'd count people who went to Episcopal colleges necessarily as well educated." Banker Thompson is a staunch Southern Baptist, and his antipathy for the southern branch of the Anglican church is well known. Many of the wealthier landowners during slavery had been Episcopalians, and the banker still harbors a lightly shrouded inferiority complex, since he is descended from a line of tradesmen who had their start traveling from town to town and from plantation to plantation by wagon, hawking all sorts of dry goods. They carried everything from bolts of cloth to cooking utensils and patent medicines. No, there was no way Banker Thompson would concede that an Episcopal college could provide a good education. As for being a war hero, well, that was just a matter of luck, wasn't it? There were plenty of good Baptist heroes as well.

He continues his criticism of the Judge. "In fact, were he truly well educated, he would have a different idea about all those nigras he has working for him." The banker has lanced the boil, and now Faulkner will have to suffer the pus and blood that such actions occasion. Not a pleasant thought at table, but there it was. It is the writer in Faulkner that causes him to compare a diatribe on race to the lancing of a boil.

"They came with his father from Alabama. It's not as if we didn't already have enough of our own former slaves here in Mississippi, but they had to bring in more from Alabama. And the way he treats them. I mean, look at that big buck he has running his timber business. Traveling around the state undercutting good, white timber men, costing them profits they need to pay back their loans to the banks. Then there's that grange he runs. Oh, don't let him tell you it's a community effort, because I know for a fact that he supplements the costs with money from his farm. Come planting or harvesting time, his people get all the good laborers to work for them. I'd say it's criminal, but he's the county judge, and that brother-in-law of his is the sheriff. I mean, he thinks we don't know that he's giving people money to pay their taxes. Why, that's like buying votes. But he gets away with it by paying out from 'shares' in that cooperative. It's strange those dividends get paid just before the taxes are due. And then he runs those trucks around the county on voting day, bringing in nigras to vote and taking them home. Well, it won't be that way too much longer. Sooner or later, the Judge is going to overextend himself supporting those people, and when he does…"

"Dear!" This from Mrs. Thompson. "I'm sure Mr. Faulkner would rather not talk politics or local scandal at dinner." Faulkner momentarily feels a warm spot in his heart for the woman until she follows with, "And I'm sure he doesn't want to talk about the nigras and all the problems they cause."

It is actually Alice who stems further pus-letting by quickly edging into the silence her mother has created with, "Mr. Faulkner, you've lived in Hollywood. Have you ever met Clark Gable? Is he as handsome in person as he is in his movies? Have you met Jean Harlow? What about Greta Garbo?"

Faulkner half expects Mrs. Thompson to once again intervene, but she does not. Looking at her face as Alice rattles off questions about Hollywood stars, Faulkner guesses correctly that she just might be as starstruck as her sixteen-year-old daughter.

Exhausting her list of stars, Alice waits. Faulkner chews the piece of pot roast he has in his mouth an extra twenty or so times before swallowing. This as an excuse not to respond to the banker's earlier comments. Then he looks across at Alice, "Why yes, Alice, I do know Clark Gable, and he is just as nice off the screen as he is on it. As for Jean Harlow, she's a real hoot." The rest of the meal is spent with Faulkner grabbing a bite here and there as he fields questions from the family about this person or that person in Hollywood. Even the banker is interested in the cowboy stars. Is it true that Hoot Gibson is a real cowboy?

At some point, Faulkner finds himself explaining the difference between on-screen roles and offscreen persona. It is only toward dessert when he discovers he might well be talking of himself when he speaks about some actors having an off-screen persona that is a role like any other. A role, played for the public, that can never be allowed to reflect the true self. A role, in fact, played to hide the true self. Many of the big stars have little peccadilloes that the studios take great pains to keep from the public. As a writer for one of the more prominent studios, Faulkner has collaborated in creating past lives for some of the stars. Lives that make it seem that either the star comes from good, wholesome, average America or has been some rakish, soldier-of-fortune adventurer. Yes, their lives are tailor-made roles that the actors play. But now he is striking too close to home.

Why, he wonders to himself, is this conversation becoming almost as difficult to handle as the one he luckily avoided on Negroes and the Judge? He is glad to finish his German chocolate cake and push back from the table. As a Baptist, the banker will not be offering him an after-lunch drink or pipes in the library. Instead, it will most likely be rocking chairs on the porch; the wind has picked up somewhat, though, and thus it seems more likely it will be a cushion on the Victorian settee in the parlor. There might even be readings from the Bible. Perhaps one of the girls will play the piano, although he has seen nothing to indicate the family is at all musical. This will be followed, somewhat later, by a cold supper from dinner's leftovers, more parlor, and then bed. Just how early can he plead lack of sleep from the previous evening's activities and get himself alone in his bedroom? Certainly, he cannot retire until at least an hour after supper. He is not sure he is up to the rigors of such an afternoon and evening. He thinks about reading the book he brought with him, Somerset Maugham's new autobiography, *A Summing Up*. Still, upon reflection, he does not remember seeing anything other than a straight-backed chair in the bedroom. Oh well, he thinks, an afternoon and evening in durance vile. I suppose it could be worse. But, in truth, he really doesn't think it could be worse. He is only trying to comfort himself. Were he a Buddhist, he would see this as a balancing of karma for his evening of foxhunting and morning breakfast with the Judge.

CHAPTER 15

THE DUNCE'S CAP

TUESDAY EVENING, LITTLE ARCH RETURNS from New Orleans with the Stinson humming like a spinning top. He brings with him the Judge's young nephew Shelby Devereux, known to family and friends as Shell but always as Shelby to his mom. Unless, of course, he is in trouble, and then it is "SHELBY ARCHIBALD DEVEREUX!" At sixteen, he is big for his age, having the height and physique of someone in his twenties. The baby fat that rounded his face not so long ago has given way to a lean, chiseled jaw, and his eyes are gray and purple, like the sun setting behind a just-passed thunderstorm. He is the youngest of the Judge's nephews and nieces, and he is also the Judge's favorite. This is probably because his mother, Fiona, is the Judge's baby sister, on whom he doted as a teenager, there being some ten years' difference in their ages. Her New Orleans home seems far away, although it is less than an hour by airplane and, in fact, with the Judge driving, just a little over two hours by car.

Shell should be in school, but like his cousin John before him, he is being schooled at home, in his case by his mother and a set of tutors. Sometimes he visits his uncle, the Judge, who runs him through his paces with the classics and conducts discussions in Italian, a language Shell is taking to almost as well as he took to French. Shell's French sounds almost native—well, as native as it can be when spoken with an Acadian accent. His French tutor, Monsieur Toussaint, works hard to remove the accent, but it is just part of Shell. His father's family owns, among other things, a sugarcane farm on one of the bayous west of New Orleans, and most of the workers are Acadian locals or immigrants from Haiti, so Shell just naturally picked up the accent. He has been to France with his father and mother on two occasions and returned each time speaking good Parisian French, but within a month or so, he always reverts to the patois of the Bayou, mixing far too much English and Spanish into his French. It drives Monsieur Toussaint to distraction. In truth, Shell can speak proper French whenever he chooses, but he enjoys his tutor's facial expressions whenever he rips off a sentence with his best Acadian accent. Although his mother tries to involve him with other young people, Shell is most at home with adults. He is neither rambunctious nor precocious; he understands when he should or should not speak or be seen.

Although Shell wasn't scheduled to come up until later in the month, he insisted on returning today with Little Arch because Little Arch lets him fly the Stinson. Shell is already an experienced pilot and passed his private-pilot's license exam and check ride on his sixteenth birthday. The Judge has announced to his friends that in a year or so, Shell will probably be one of the better pilots in Louisiana and Mississippi. He is a natural stick-and-rudder man, the Judge tells his friends but only when he is out of earshot of Shell. "No sense in making the child any cockier than he already is," the Judge confides. But quietly he is proud of Shell, just as he is of his son, John, and his adopted son, Joshua. Next month Shell will travel to Europe to spend Christmas with his cousin John in Germany. It is time, the Judge thinks, that Shell sees for himself the consequences of following demagogues. If he had just been a little older, he could have experienced demagoguery firsthand during Huey Long's reign in his home state. From time to time, the Judge has pointed out the similarities between Huey, Hitler, and Mussolini, but Shell is just now at an age where he can begin to appreciate such comparisons. And, of course, the Judge awaits the moment when Shell will ask him if he himself is not a demagogue. Of course, Shell will never ask the Judge, because he already knows.

Wednesday afternoon finds the two on the porch rocking. Tristan and Iseult are sprawled in the slanting-but-still-warm November sun. It is, after all, southern Mississippi, and even November afternoons occasion only the need for shirtsleeves or cotton jackets at the most.

"Uncle Arch, I understand you entertained Mr. William Faulkner for breakfast on Saturday." Shell rocks next to his uncle on the high front porch.

"Did that," his uncle grunts, pipestem in his mouth as he fishes deep into the pocket of his canvas blazer for his tobacco pouch. Pulling it out, he continues. "If I had known you were coming up early, I'd have had you fetch up this tobacco, since the shop isn't that far from your father's New Orleans house. Instead, it came up with the package courier for Mr. Ledbetter's store."

"I would've been happy to bring it up. By the way, that tobacco does have a nice smell to it. Does it taste as good as it smells?" Shell draws in a deep breath of the smoke that has floated under his nose.

The Judge, having just lit a new bowl, puffs twice and then hands the pipe to Shell. "Have a puff. Remember, draw it deep into your lungs or you won't get the effect."

Taking the pipe, a first for Shell, he puts the tip between his lips and sucks in. His mouth fills with smoke that travels down his windpipe and up into his nose. It burns. When it reaches his lungs, he feels as if he is going to spontaneously combust from the inside out. And his nose, then his sinuses, seems on fire as well. The Judge takes the pipe from Shell's hand then slams his other hand against his back.

"Breathe; don't hold it in," he instructs.

This is, of course, an instruction Shell does not need, for he is trying to expel the smoke as quickly as possible, blowing out through his nose and mouth with a whooshing sound like a strong wind making the turn at the corner of a house. And then he coughs—and coughs. He rises from the chair and walks from one corner of the porch to the other coughing. After three or four minutes, he manages to catch his breath and gingerly settles back into the chair.

"Well, does it?" the Judge asks.

"Does it what?" Shell croaks out, his voice a ragged imitation of a bullfrog.

"Does it taste as good as it smells?"

"Ha ha," Shell tries to say, but it comes out more as *Cha—* *cough*—*cha*. He is not impressed with the object lesson.

"Shall we discuss hell today?" The Judge, of course, is referring to the underworld of Greek mythology ruled by Hades. Specifically, he wants Shell to explain the concept of "Shades" and why everybody in the classical Greek world ends up in Hades.

The dogs sense it first, their heads coming up, followed slowly and then more quickly by their lean bodies. They move to the edge of the porch, looking north. In a minute or so, a red-dust plume appears over the tops of the pine trees to the north of the house. Shortly thereafter, a car and a pickup truck turn off the red-dirt road onto the pea-gravel drive. They crunch their way up the drive, each skidding ever so slightly as they stop in front of the steps to the house.

Shell recognizes the sheriff's 1936 Dodge in no small part because it has a red spotlight on the side and a large six-pointed star on the door that says "Sheriff." He does not recognize the pickup, although he can tell it's a 1936 or 1937 Chevy half ton. Both vehicles are black, but the mud-splattered fenders and doors of the pickup make it seem older than it really is.

The Judge remains seated as the sheriff climbs out of his vehicle and opens the back door to the Dodge. He orders two young men out of the back seat. Their hands are cuffed behind them. Then, from the front seat, the sheriff extracts a young lady. She too is handcuffed, but her cuffs are in the front. As she approaches the porch with her head down, she looks like a pious penitent walking into church fearful of the hell-and-brimstone sermon she is about to endure.

A deputy sheriff emerges from the cab of the pickup. At over six feet, he is too tall to wear his Stetson in the cab, so he stops for a moment to place it on his head and adjust it carefully. Then, hoisting up his gun belt, he steps onto the running board and reaches into the back of the pickup. He withdraws two large Mason jars from one of several boxes in the bed of the truck. Jars in hand, he takes his place behind the handcuffed miscreants.

"Morning, Arch." The sheriff is the only person besides Miss Julia who calls the Judge "Arch." Everyone else in the county calls him Judge or Uncle Arch.

"Morning, Cleveland." The Judge addresses his brother-in-law, for Cleveland is Miss Julia's older brother. His tenure as sheriff is only slightly shorter than the Judge's length of service as the county magistrate. They are both kept in office by a voting bloc of independent small-scale farmers, sharecroppers, and Negroes in no small part because the sheriff assures the safety of the voting precincts in the county on Election Day and the co-op provides transportation to and from the polling places.

"Arch," the sheriff continues, "we found Jim Bob, Buford, and Sissy here over on the CCC road with several boxes of these in the bed of their truck." He points to the deputy, who holds up the Mason jars. "We likely wouldn't have caught them if they hadn't run up behind Fred Harmon dragging a cultivator back to his barn. That Chevy has a souped-up engine in it."

The deputy comes up the steps and hands one of the jars to the Judge, who opens it, sniffs it, and sticks his finger first into the clear liquid and then into his mouth. Smelling the liquid in the jar once more, the Judge asks, "How much did you boys pay Old Man Billingsworth for this 'shine?" He looks down from his chair to the boys standing eight feet below him.

"Didn't pay nobody nothing. Ain't ours." This is from the taller of the two, Jim Bob Gilbert from the Gilbert clan over near Homestead. At six feet, his head is still two feet below the edge of the porch, so he has to crane his neck to look up at the Judge. "Besides, it ain't 'shine; it's cleaning fluid for carburetors. Fellers over at the garage use it to soak grease and such from engine parts."

"Why, Jim Bob! I see dropping out of high school hasn't hurt you any. That's a most attractive cover story for possessing...what have we got here?" The Judge stands and walks to the edge of the porch, where he can see into the bed of the pickup. "Must be about forty or fifty quarts of good old American corn whiskey. See, you would use denatured alcohol for cleaning your engine parts, and this is just good old ethanol made from corn mash. If you'd stayed in school, you would know that. And here's the other problem with your story: if this was denatured alcohol to clean engine parts, you wouldn't be running around carrying it in one-quart Mason jars. You'd have it in larger containers, and they probably wouldn't be as nice and clean as these Mason jars are." He reaches the jar down to the deputy, who is, once again, standing behind the boys.

"Now, Miss Sissy, I don't believe you're sixteen yet. Is that right?"

The girl, tears in her eyes, looks up into the Judge's. "No sir, I won't be sixteen 'til next February."

"Do your parents know you're out with these boys?" The Judge is squatting down at the edge of the porch. His sweat-stained Stetson is pushed back on his head. He looks almost fatherly as he speaks to the girl.

"No sir, they think I'm at Judith Gaskin's house crushing grapes and pressing apples for Mrs. Gaskin's cordials and cider."

Were these not serious circumstances, the Judge might almost be amused by the irony of legal grape and apple alcohol versus the illicit corn alcohol in the back of the truck, but he does not smile as he stands and walks over to the steps and then down to the gravel drive. He takes Sissy by the shoulder and leads her off in front of the Dodge, where he has quiet words. After a few minutes, in which Sissy's tears become shoulder-shuddering sobs, he motions for the sheriff to remove her handcuffs and then leaves her standing, head hanging and arms at her sides in front of the large car. He steps over to the pickup and, reaching into the bed, pulls the tarp covering the boxes all the way out of the truck. Just behind the cab of the truck is a longish cardboard box, its four-paneled top tucked closed. He opens it, reaches in, and pulls out two long, white, pointed hats.

At first, Shell, who is watching from the porch, thinks them dunces' caps. He has seen numerous illustrations of poorly performing students condemned to the corner stool with a tall, pointed paper hat on which has been printed "Dunce" or "Fool." But he quickly changes his assessment as he notes the cloth flaps hanging from the front and back of the caps. One flap is longish, as though it goes down the back as a short cape, and the short front flap is a face mask with eyeholes. Uh oh, he thinks. Klan hats. Uncle Arch is not going to be happy. He had thought he might go inside, but the urge to watch what happens is too great, and he sits quietly in his chair.

The Judge throws the hats up on the edge of the porch and confronts the two young men.

"Boys, I had intended to let you off with a fifty-dollar fine for being stupid enough to run 'shine in the daytime, but Miss Sissy tells me you might have been having your way with her. Now, both of you being over eighteen makes it suspicion of sexual misconduct, maybe even rape. I don't know. We'll have to have the sheriff investigate, but while that's happening, you'll both be in jail awhile."

He turns to the sheriff. "Take Sissy to town and have Doctor Whatley check her over. You know what to tell him to look for. Then take her to your office and get her statement. Have a deputy go out to her daddy's farm and advise her parents to come and get her. Take the boys to the county jail and lock them up. They're both over eighteen, so we don't have to notify anyone. I'll be in presently to do the paper work and call the district attorney. If anybody asks, tell them bail hasn't been set, but you think it'll be at least five thousand dollars each." Halfway back up the stairs to the porch, he turns.

"Impound the truck as county property for transporting illegal liquor. We'll sell it at auction, and their families can buy it back if they want."

Back up on the porch, he looks down at the two boys. At over six-three in his boots and looking down off the eight-foot porch, he towers over them as Solomon might have over the biblical women when he ordered the child divided. The Judge speaks softly, his baritone voice low enough that both accused have to tilt not only their necks but also their backs to see and hear him. He pronounces, "Jim Bob Gilbert, Buford Simon, you are under arrest for bootlegging and suspicion of sexual knowledge of a minor." Reaching down, he scoops up the two hats, and his baritone voice becomes stentorian in its strength and volume.

"I want the two of you to know, and I want you to tell your friends and kin, that you don't do this sort of thing in this county." From the manner in which he waves the hats in front of them, it is easy to understand that his admonition is meant more as an antiklan censure than as a caution against bootlegging and sex with minors.

He dismisses the two with a wave of his hand and strides to the other end of the porch, where he stops and looks out over the outbuildings and the now-fallow fields to the west. The sheriff herds the two boys back into the Dodge, while Sissy is instructed to ride with the deputy in the pickup.

As the red-dust cloud from the two vehicles dissipates, the Judge paces the length of the porch a few times. Shell remains frozen in place, fearing to move from his chair. Finally, the

Judge announces, "Well, we have to be about our purpose now, don't we, Shell?" He snatches up the two hats from where he had dropped them and, bounding down the porch, says, "Let's go down to the barn."

They stop at the barn only long enough to collect a small can of gasoline, and then they head into the field where the farm keeps a fire pit to dispose of refuse and other farm detritus. The Judge throws the two hats onto the pile that is awaiting disposal, douses them with gasoline, and touches the flame of his trench lighter to the tip of one of the cones. They catch quickly. In two or three seconds, both hats blaze up into the darkening afternoon sky. As they burn, the Judge loudly proclaims in Latin, "*Vade! Draco maledicti et omnis legio diabolica, exorcizamos te!*" (Be gone! Evil dragon and all your diabolical legions, we exorcize you!)

The two pieces of starched cotton burn quickly, and thus the klan is again dispossessed, just as the church exorcizes demons. The Judge does not like the klan, and the klan does not like the Judge.

"Now, Shell, let's go get some hot tea and talk about Hades and who should go there—in the Christian sense and not the classical."

The two walk back to the house, the dogs at their heels.

CHAPTER 16

A LETTER FROM FAULKNER

THE JUDGE READS THE FIRST paragraph of Faulkner's letter to Miss Julia:

> Dear Judge and Miss Julia,
>   My sincerest apologies for the lateness of this note, but I had to deal with some unexpected issues that my publisher raised about my next novel, *The Wild Palms*, which is due out in January.

After another pleasantry or two, the paragraph ends with:

> Judge, I have to agree with you that Miss Julia's biscuits are far and away the best I've ever had, but her pear preserves make them truly a food for the gods.

Here, Faulkner has drawn a small loving cup sitting atop a mountain. There are small circles, which the Judge takes to be biscuits, falling from the top of the loving cup. He shows the page to Miss Julia, who remarks, "Good thing Mr. Faulkner is a writer and not an artist."

Taking the page back, the Judge silently reads the rest of the letter.

> I truly enjoyed our conversation. It is unusual in this day and age to find a man as free with his informed opinions as you. My afternoon and evening with the Thompson family, while not so diverting as my visit with you, were nonetheless instructive, but in a rather disappointing way.
>
> I suppose my time in Hollywood has given me a different perspective from which to consider my home state, and I do have to say that such a new perspective can lead to disconcerting perceptions. On the one hand, it is difficult to understand the corruption of Christian principles that has occurred in Mississippi. On the other, it is almost totally understandable, if regrettable. Perhaps it is that I understand but wish I didn't.
>
> Yet, while perhaps not as open but still very much real, the same difference of the races exists in Hollywood. In the South, it is open hostility, while in Hollywood, it is cloaked. My travels north of the Mason-Dixon Line have shown me that the same

cloaked segregation of color exists there as well, with the Negroes forced into their own communities. It is only in the rural South that Negroes and whites live in such proximity.

I sometimes wonder whether the situation might be different if Lincoln had not been assassinated. Still, he was responsible for more American deaths than all the other presidents combined, including those deaths of the Great War. And now, if your predictions are correct, Roosevelt will have us join a great crusade that can end only in the deaths of thousands more Americans. Is it mankind's destiny to destroy itself? Do you really think war is the inevitable outcome of the current European crisis?

As for your situation with—how did you call them—the cavaliers of the New South? I would be very interested in learning more, for I think there is the potential for an extremely good novel within the material. The real question is, do I have the courage to write such a novel? And, as you noted, there is as yet no ending. Still, I think there's a good story there.

The Wild Palms is what I refer to as a contrapuntal story—that is, two different stories woven together with alternating chapters, as with a piece of music that has two distinct melodies that complement each other. I'm pretty happy with the effect, and I think the second story, "Old Man," is one of my better pieces of writing. Please let me know what you think. I've asked the publisher to send you a reviewer's copy.

Time wants to do a piece on me that will come out with the book. They're sending a fellow down early next month to interview me. He's coming from New York, but they tell me he is originally from the state of Washington. Doubt he'll know much about the South—and what he does know will probably have to be retaught.

Again, thank you for your hospitality, and please let me know what you think of *The Wild Palms*. My best to you both.

Sincerely,
William Faulkner

He had stricken through *William* and, in cursive, written *Bill*. The rest of the letter was typed. That he had typed his name and then written *Bill* in cursive seemed to the Judge yet another affectation.

CHAPTER 17

THE PLAN

"IT'S A CLEARING OFF THE fire road near the county line, just north of the turnoff to the old Carson place. Pretty near where the river flood left that Oxbow Lake in '27. Going to be a big one. Some state big shots are going to attend. Seems you're going to be one of the people they speak against. Something about getting you out of office one way or another." Jesse puffed his pipe twice to keep it lit.

"Hmm" was the only reply the Judge gave. He seemed deep in thought.

"They're sure enough after you, Arch. If I was you, I'd watch my back real careful-like."

"Jesse, I've been watching my back since 1917. It's a combat-pilot thing. Watch your back, but always watch the sun as well. Because while you're looking behind you, they might be coming at you out of that bright sun in front of you. That's why the dawn patrols were so dangerous in the war. Our pilots were flying east into the rising sun, and their aircraft were coming out of that sun. They'd see us long before we could see them. So, I always flew with two pair of goggles—one with smoked lenses for flying into the sun and one with clear lenses for cloudy days or flying in the evening. But you're right; it does seem time to do something, although I have to be in New Orleans next weekend." The Judge craned his neck around from his chair to find Shell at the other end of the store.

"Shell, if you're through coveting a new Barlow knife, I reckon we should be getting home." He pushed himself up from the rocker and put out his hand. "Thanks, Jesse, and I will watch my back, but you be careful too. If any of the klan find out you tell me these things, they'll be real upset."

Jesse rose more slowly than the Judge, his arthritis rebelling against the cold, damp, late-fall Mississippi morning.

"Don't need those kind of people 'round here anymore. Nothing but trouble—grand dragons and kleagles and such. Nothing but hooligans dressed up like ghosts to scare the Negroes."

"Yes, well, hooligans, dressed up or not, are still dangerous, so you be careful."

The Judge and Jesse shake hands, and then the Judge takes his leather coat from the back of the rocking chair and puts it on. It is a lighter version of the one he wore in the cockpit of his DH-4 in 1918. This one doesn't have the shearling lining, but it does have the high collar and midthigh length of the original. There is no need, at any time of the year, in Mississippi for a shearling-lined coat, but since the Judge always drives his Packard with the top down unless, of course, it is raining, the leather coat is ideal for breaking the wind that comes over the windscreen and resisting the cold that comes with it. Shell is wearing his hunting field jacket but has a sweater underneath, and he has a hunter's cap with earflaps that turn down over his ears. As the screen door swings shut behind them, the Judge asks, "How about you drive us home?"

Shell, not so tall as the Judge, has to move the seat up some to reach the pedals on the floor, but otherwise he is the spitting image of his uncle. He drives the big car with what he feels is the same abandon, but a shrewd observer would notice more slowing as he enters curves and slower acceleration as he comes out of them. Still, an average driver he is not. He handles the car with an instinctive ability for all things moving, and living in three dimensions is no problem for him.

"Shell, you've got to go home sooner than I thought. You and Joshua can fly down next Thursday in the Stinson. I'll bring your aunt in the car, and we can visit with your mother and father over the weekend." The Judge waits until they have arrived in front of the house again to further open up the conversation. "I'll make it up to you by giving you acrobatic lessons on the Stearman next spring." The Judge refers to the open-cockpit two-seater he keeps in the hangar. He made an emotional purchase of it at an auction in Ohio in 1935. It had belonged to a farmer near Lima who lost his holdings to a bank when his crops failed. Several other farmers in the area had lost their farms, and there was a lot of equipment for sale. The Judge had traveled north looking for a decent tractor to buy and had returned with not only a newish tractor but the airplane as well. Unlike the enclosed cockpit of the Stinson, the Stearman provided an experience similar to the DH-4. The Judge enjoyed flying it, and it—along with the Packard—was one of his few indulgences. Well, and perhaps his foxhounds.

"Hmm…" Shell considers the offer. "And I can use the Stinson when I take the examination for my instructor pilot's license?"

Although the Judge had always considered that arrangement a given, he agrees it can be part of the bargain, and Shell is satisfied. He knows his uncle would not suggest something if it wasn't necessary. He suspects it has something to do with the discussion with Mr. Ledbetter back at the store, for he had overheard snippets of the conversation, and he was pretty sure it had to do with the klan.

Thus, on Thursday, Little Arch and Shell fly the Stinson to the New Orleans airport. They leave just after breakfast. Shell said his good-byes to Tristan and Iseult, who had to be kept in the house or they would have followed him to the airstrip below the barn. Shell wears his field jacket again, because even in the comfort of the Stinson cabin, the heater smells like burning gasoline and oil, and it is better to leave it off. It is time, Shell thinks, to get himself a leather flying coat. He will ask his father to make that his Christmas gift this year. Perhaps it should come early, since he will be in Germany for Christmas. Berlin in December could be mighty cold.

Before leaving with Miss Julia in the Packard, the Judge meets with his brother-in-law.

"Cleveland, can you have some of your nonklan deputies over here tomorrow night? I understand I'm to be reviled and pilloried at the big klan gathering, and some of the more violent types might think burning us out is a good idea. I imagine they'll have to get pretty well liquored-up before they'll do anything, but it is Friday night, and there'll be a lot of rabble-rousing at the meeting. I understand they're bringing in a dragon or two from Jackson and elsewhere. Maybe you could deputize some other of our local antiklan constituents. I also want you to protect all the Negroes. I know it's a big job, but I have something in mind that may help tamp down the eagerness of the night riders."

The sheriff looks pained. He too knows about the klan rally and the visiting bigwigs. Even given the seriousness of the situation, he almost smiles when he thinks of the origin of the term *bigwigs*. Maybe the klan bigwigs should more appropriately be referred to as tall coneheads.

"I've been thinking along the same lines," he replies. "I have five deputies I can depend on, so I'll put each of them in charge of a group of temporary deputies. I can get all five of the Johnson boys, and there're the Tadlocks and the Smiths over at High Hill. I'll have enough. By the way, are you going to share with me that you plan to interfere in their joyriding?"

The Judge considers a moment and then answers, "Not today. If it succeeds, it will be apparent enough. If not, your boys will need to be ready. Thompson and his ilk really want to break up the co-op, and we can't let them do it." The Judge puts on his dress Stetson and calls for Miss Julia.

The Packard, its top up, pulls out of the driveway and heads for New Orleans.

"Julia, Arch! Come in!" Fiona greets her brother and sister-in-law with hugs. At five-eight, she is tall for a woman but still barely reaches her brother's shoulder. The two are in time for a late lunch, and the three of them are joined by Fiona's husband, Eugene.

"So, to what do we owe this surprise visit?" Eugene asks as the maid brings in the soup tureen.

"Something I would rather discuss after lunch," the Judge replies, as he applies a butter knife to a piece of a yeast roll.

"Oh, go on and tell the man we're here because the klan is having a big meeting tomorrow night and you don't think it's safe at home." Miss Julia has no qualms about discussing the klan over soup and filet of sole. And when the Judge gives her a disbelieving look, she continues, "What, you think I'm blind and deaf? Why, Arch Cameron, I know almost as much about what's going on in the county as you. You don't think Abigail and Winona's people know what the klan is doing? They absolutely do. They've sent some of their younger children and grandchildren to visit relatives in other parts of the state, and some of them have come down here too. Now you tell Eugene what it is you plan to do, because I know you don't intend to stay here and cede any kind of control to the ku kluxers."

Appropriately chastised, the Judge leans back in his chair and wipes soup from his chin with his napkin. He needs a moment to regain his composure, for this moment is a bit of a primordial revelation for him. He has always known Julia knew more than she let on, but for her to know this much is a surprise. Still, twenty-five years of marriage can teach a wife a lot about her spouse, and apparently Julia has been learning all the time.

"Well, Eugene, Julia is right. I do have a plan. I left Cleveland with instructions about defending against the devil's hordes if they actually reach their intended targets—one of which I'm sure is my farm. My plan is to keep them from reaching those targets, but I'll need your help on a short time frame."

"Arch, you may have whatever I have, and I, personally, am at your service" is Eugene's only reply.

"Thank you." The Judge leans left toward Eugene, and they begin a tête-à-tête, the Judge occasionally gesturing with his hands in the manner of an experienced pilot describing this jink and that zag.

CHAPTER 18

THE BURNING CROSS

AT THREE O'CLOCK IN THE afternoon on Friday, a pickup leaves New Orleans headed north to Mississippi. It carries in its bed a number of one-by-four pine boards painted black and rust red, several large bags of Spanish moss and dried sphagnum moss, and a cardboard box not unlike the one that had carried Shell's "dunces" caps. Eugene drives, and the Judge rides in the passenger seat. But it does not seem to be the Judge unless you look closely, for he is wearing a fake mustache, a wig, and a pair of heavy, black-rim glasses. It would not do for the local boys to recognize him.

They wear sidearms, and across the back of the window hangs a short-barrel Remington 12-gauge pump shotgun and a Winchester .30-30 lever-action rifle. Both are loaded.

"We pray in the name of Jesus Christ, our God and Savior. Amen!"

"Aaaamen!" the klatch of klansmen echoes, the sound reverberating through the pine trees as the klan kludd finishes the invocation to the meeting. The twenty-foot-high pitch-covered cross had been lit before dark and now completely fills the clearing as the primary source of light. A few of the robed klansmen hold torches and some have set camping and hunting lanterns on the hoods of the cars and pickups that are parked on the periphery of the circle around the cross. There are more than two hundred white-robed and white-hooded men in attendance. Sprinkled here and there are some green robes, while standing on the bed of a flatbed truck backed in near, but not too near, the cross are three individuals who wear red shiny robes with the insignia of a Maltese cross inside a circle. These are the king kleagle, the regional klaliff, and the cyclops of the klan, and it is they who do the speaking—or rather, yelling, for they do not speak as orators but more as hooligans in chief ratcheting the mob into a bloodlust. They could be Bolsheviks outside the Kremlin in 1918 or Jacobins in front of the Bastille in 1789. But, in truth, they are more like leaders of the Nazi Sturmabteilung and Schutzstaffel, who only weeks before had stormed through German cities burning and despoiling Jewish homes and businesses. The three klan leaders shout threats against the Negroes, the Catholics, the Jews, and all their supposed henchmen, naming, in particular, the Judge. They tell the rest of the klansmen how these people deny them their rightful shares of prosperity, how they threaten the Christian morality, and how they will continue to do so until driven from the county, the state, and the nation. Just like their goose-stepping cousins on the continent, they preach hate, and their listeners love it.

By the time the third speaker, a kleagle from Jackson, finishes his inciting, the mob is ready to launch upon their great crusade to rid the county of undesirables. They literally leap to their cars and trucks, eager to do the bidding of their capuchin-wearing masters. Lesser klan officers yell "Follow me!" as they lead the vehicles of their "wrecking crews" down the fire lane that leads back to the main road. Many have cans of gasoline and unlit torches in the beds of their trucks. Some have chains and rope. The stream of vehicles moves fast, leaving, after a few minutes, only the klan nighthawk, responsible for dousing the cross, and the red-robed leaders in the clearing.

"I would be honored if you would spend the night at my house," the klaliff offers the visiting kleagle from Jackson. "I suppose you have heard that William Faulkner stayed with me last month." This, he thinks, just might impress the kleagle, but, in fact, it has the opposite effect.

"Isn't Faulkner that degenerate writer from Oxford who allows the white children in his books to play with the nigra children and treats them as equal characters? No, I don't think I would care to sleep in the same bed as someone who professes to the world that whites are equals with the nigras. Thank you all the same. Besides, if I were you, I'd go someplace very public so that you can, when asked, disassociate yourself from any violence that may occur tonight. Those of us who lead the cause cannot be trapped into having our reputations besmirched by something some white-trash crack-er might take it in his head to do."

And with that as his parting, he leaves the three now cone-less klansmen standing in the dying light of the cross. Their elongated shadows mingle with that of the cross, so that a pho-tograph would show three bodies hung beneath its eastward-pointing arm.

While the kleagle, cyclops, and klaliff wind up their explosive clock, the Judge and Eugene busily set out the one-by-fours. A very close inspection shows that the boards have small nails, also painted black, protruding from one face. The nails are ran-domly placed, but a rubber tire running over one of the boards will receive one, two, or perhaps even three small punctures. Not so large a puncture as to cause a blowout but certainly large enough to precipitate a small leak in the tube inside the tire. The Judge and Eugene place several of the boards on the track leading out of the clearing and cover each with strands of moss. In the black of the moonless night, none of the boards on the road are visible, and vehicles crossing them will find them no rougher than any other section of the mostly unused fire lane. If anyone observes the two men laying out the boards, they see only two white-robed klansmen on the track.

It is not unusual for there to be guards posted along the approach to a large meeting site, and for this meeting there are two sets of guards—one set at the turnoff from the county road and one at the entrance to the clearing. It is between these sets of guards that the Judge and Eugene place the boards. They place boards nearest the clearing first, and then they wait until the kleagle is just about finished with his diatribe. As the meeting ends, they drive by the guards at the turnoff, and Eugene yells at them, "Better get back to your wrecking crews; they're ready to roll."

As the guards attempt to run while holding up the hems of their robes and grabbing to keep their cones on their heads, the Judge and Eugene laugh, wishing they could have photographs of the flailing klansmen, or, as the Judge describes them, klownsmen. After they round the final bend of the track as they depart, the Judge and Eugene place a remaining board across its entrance. In all, they put down twelve boards in different spots on the track, which is so narrow that it is impossible to drive around the boards.

Only two or three of the vehicles escape the Judge's plan of action unscathed, and when those vehicles arrive at the Judge's farm, they are met by the sheriff and a group of ten stern-looking men carrying shotguns. The sheriff, using his knowledge of the locals, calls many of them by name, for he, too, knows the tricks of identification. None of these people have been smart enough to change the pants, boots, or shoes that protrude from the hems of their robes. A few wear recognizable rings, and a couple have unique wristwatches. It matters not that their faces are covered, for the sheriff knows them all from their boots or pants and even, in some cases, from their eyes, which he can see through the holes in their masks. Hearing themselves called by name—along, of course, with being confronted by the ten shotguns—is enough to dampen their ardor for mayhem. But perhaps it is the thought of a county-jail sentence assigned by the very Judge whose house they want to torch that is enough to dampen the fire in the head, if not the heart, of even the most ardent klansman. Then too, of course, the sight of the shotguns move their stomachs with the fear that only shotguns can instill.

The Judge and Eugene do not see their handiwork, but dawn finds cars and trucks scattered on the sides of roads and highways throughout the county. Most of the owners had one spare tire, but none had more than one, so the cars remain stranded until other tires and tubes can be found.

On Tuesday, someone from the klan finally inspects the meeting site and the fire lanes. Of course, they discover the nail-studded boards, but only after driving across them on the way in to the meeting site. More deflated tires result. When the guards from the meeting are questioned, they swear that none but klan members passed in from the road, and so there is great mystery as to who sabotaged the site. Everyone knows it couldn't have been the Judge or the sheriff, for the former had been in New Orleans—this was confirmed by klan members in the city—and the latter had been at the Judge's farm when the surviving vehicles, one of which eventually had three tires go flat during the confrontation with the sheriff, had arrived.

Who, then, had betrayed the klan? An investigation would prove futile, and the county klan would receive a major black eye in the state and national organization for leaving the Jackson kleagle stranded on the highway. And that kleagle, in an attempt to divert attention from his participation in the event, had accused the regional klaliff of consorting by personally entertaining a degenerate Hollywood writer.

The Judge, though, had enjoyed a delightful weekend with his sister and brother-in-law, attending mass at Christ Church Cathedral on Sunday morning and returning to Mississippi later that evening. The sheriff had enjoyed a quiet weekend, although his deputies were busy tagging a number of vehicles with abandoned vehicle tickets for being left driverless on the sides of diverse county roads. The other people in the county who were happiest that weekend were the tire dealers and service stations that were open on Saturday. The county literally ran out of tire tubes and patches, and trips to Jackson and Hattiesburg were necessary to procure sufficient replacements. Since the cars were scattered all over the western end of the county, many of them hadn't been serviced before Monday or Tuesday.

The story, which would be told and retold in every venue of the state, would take on the status of both mystical saga and deep mystery. But no local Nancy Drew or Hardy Boy would ever solve the mystery of the punctured pride and tires of the ku klukkers. Some would say the investigators were "kluless," and the story would provide a great laugh for many who feared, loathed, and otherwise despised the klukkers, who, it was hoped, would someday incinerate themselves at one of their cross burnings.

CHAPTER 19

CHRISTMAS 1938

AFTER THE HORRIBLE EVENTS OF Kristallnacht in Germany, the Judge, Eugene, and Fiona considered not sending Shell to Germany. But after much soul searching and spirited debate, they eventually decided that it was in his best interest to make the trip. John would be there to protect him, and Shell would have a chance to learn how evil can be masked with good manners and strong-sounding but flawed idealism. Of course, Shell could learn that at home, but such lessons are better learned objectively when actions don't have to be disentangled from the personalities of people who are already known.

Shell recorded his thoughts in his journal. "Only girls keep diaries," he once told an acquaintance, "but men record their thoughts in a journal."

December 10, 1938. Still at sea. This German ship is much different than any of the French or British ships I've sailed on before. It is very regimented. It is good, though, because I can practice some of the German I have been studying. My reading skills are better than my speaking.

Weather out is cold and windy; better to stay inside. Seven days is a long time to be onboard a ship. Tomorrow we land in Hamburg. Discovered copy of *Master and Mate* magazine in ship's library. Interesting article by the head of the American Federation of Labor calling for a boycott of German goods. It's the December 1938 copy, so I wonder if it has reached Berlin yet? John to meet me at pier. I'll ask him about this boycott thing. Must remember to send Mother cable upon safe arrival.

December 11. Long trip; disembarked only to stand in slow-moving line for immigration. First thing I noticed was the swastika armbands and intimidating military-like uniforms of the customs and immigration officers. They were very stern in both visage and manner. One would not say they were welcoming in the least.

The people in front of me in line were Americans from Wisconsin. I overheard them say they were "returning to the Fatherland." I did not meet them on the ship, so they must have been in the second-class cabins, which had their own dining room and such. Need to give some thought to what "returning to the Fatherland" means. I'll ask John.

Immigration officer was very cold at first. Didn't seem to like the fact that I was an American. He decidedly didn't like that I couldn't speak German, but his English, while very stilted, wasn't bad. Then he asked me what the purpose of my trip was, and I told him that I was visiting my cousin, who was in Germany studying German. He asked me why John was studying German, and I told him that John thought German was going to be an important language in the future. All of a sudden, he was very nice. He smiled and immediately stamped my passport, wishing me a pleasant visit to Germany.

John was there to meet me. Train trip from Hamburg to Berlin was uneventful. Lots of soldiers and people in uniforms. The uniforms are different; some are gray, some black, and some brown, but all have the ubiquitous swastika armband. Even boys my age are wearing uniforms. John tells me they are members of the Hitler Youth. Perhaps I'll meet some of them while I'm here.

I asked John about the family who said they were returning to Germany, and he says there are many Americans returning to Germany from Midwestern states like Wisconsin, Michigan, and Ohio. He says many of them were members of the German American Bund, and their families had immigrated to the United States after the First World War. Now, because of the Depression, many of them are returning to what they believe is a revitalized Germany.

December 12. Slept late. Very tired from the long day yesterday. John's apartment is nice; it is on the second floor, which would be the third floor in New Orleans, and has a view of a park from the living room. I have my own bedroom. He left me a note saying he had an early meeting but would return before lunch. He left me some biscuits and ham, and there was coffee in the pot on the stove. The ham tasted different than our ham at home. It wasn't smoked and tasted more of salt.

Of course, we get our ham from Father's farm, so I shouldn't expect the same taste.

I spent the rest of the morning studying a map of Berlin and looking out the window into the park in front of John's apartment. I tried to count the number of people who passed wearing brown uniforms of one sort or another but lost count several times. What is it with the uniforms? Those not wearing uniforms are uniformly wearing black—black overcoats and hats mostly; there's no color in the city that I can see other than the bright-red armbands and the same red-and-black swastikas on flags hanging from many of the buildings.

December 13. Over breakfast, John and I discussed the political situation. He says things are very bad. Since Germany annexed Austria and the German-speaking part of Czechoslovakia, things haven't gotten better in the rest of Europe as Herr Hitler promised. John is sure there is going to be a war here—in Europe, I mean. He is not going to stay another six months, as he had planned, but is coming home with me in March. He wants me to learn as much German as I can while I'm here, so he has signed me up with an instructor for a crash course in German.

December 14. Herr Hitler, Herr Hitler, Heil Hitler—it is never-ending. He is in the newspapers, on the radio, and, most importantly, on the lips of everyone. John and I sit and listen in coffee bars, and all the talk is of Herr Hitler and what he has done for Germany. John translates for me. Today John and I took a taxi through a part of town that is Jewish, and I was amazed to see all the boarded-up windows. The few people in the streets, all dressed in black, looked cowed: heads down, hats tightly pulled over their eyes while they clutched their coats closed. They looked like they expected to be beaten at any moment. I can only describe their movement as scurrying—as if they did not want to be outside. John says the windows are the result of Kristallnacht, and while the destruction and loss of business is bad, what is worse is the number of Jews who were arrested and sent to concentration camps. I have seen people arrested before; it happens all the time in the French Quarter, especially to drunks. I have seen belligerent drunks beaten with police sticks, but the people in the French Quarter don't scurry from doorway to doorway expecting that any second they'll feel the wallop of a baton or the thud of a rock thrown by some boy wearing a Hitler Youth uniform. I wonder if this is how slavery was? I'll ask Uncle Arch; he remembers what Granddaddy told him about slavery.

December 20. Very busy the last few days learning German. Instructor says I'm a natural student. Ha! He just wants a tip.

Bought a copy of Faulkner's *Pylon* in German at a bookstore near the Brandenburg Gate. The title in German is *Wendermarke.* I'll take it to Uncle Arch. He can send it to Mr. Faulkner. I wonder if he has seen his books in German? They also had *Absalom, Absalom!* I'm getting much better in German. My greetings, partings, and basic conversational topics (for example, the weather, food, travel, and so on) are almost perfect, but German is nothing like French. I'm used to pursing my lips for French, and now I have to grunt and almost spit to get the German words to sound right. Still, I'm understanding a lot more than I thought I might. It helps that John and I spend a great deal of time in public venues. I'll guess at conversations I hear, and John will tell me if I'm right. He makes me do all the ordering of meals and greetings and such, helping me only if I reach a complete impasse and am unable to navigate around it using the German I know.

December 22. Met some Hitler Youth today. John and I had gone to a youth-movement meeting as guests of one of his German contacts. All I can say about these youth is that they are very taken with themselves. I couldn't understand a lot of the conversations, but there was one boy there who spoke English. His name is Ernst. He is one of the returning Americans, and he is very proud to be German, he told me. He said that in Germany, der Führer would never allow the things that are happening in the United States. Here in Germany, he said, his father has a job, and his mother can stay at home with his sister, although she insists on helping the local ladies' auxiliary. Ernst says he is already a Scharführer in the Hitler Youth, and he wants to join the Nazi Party when he is eligible. I suppose Scharführer is some kind of leadership rank, but I'm not sure. Anyway, all the boys were about my age. Some a little older, and a few younger, but all of them very stern in their bearing. None seemed to have much of a sense of humor, except I did hear some of them making what seemed to be jokes about "der Juden." I did not ask my American Nazi about the comments, for, in truth, I really didn't want to know; yet I feel guilty that I didn't ask, for I need to learn as much as I can. I didn't ask because I think they might have expected me to laugh, and I do not think I could have. In fact, I'm afraid I did understand the intent of the jokes just by the tone of the tellers, and I not only would not have laughed but am sure my face would have indicated my indignation at such things. I do not much like these Hitler Youth any more than most of the other people I've encountered who are wearing uniforms. I feel as if I'm living in an armed camp of psychopaths pretending to live in a world scripted by Wagner. Of the small knowledge I have of Germanic mystical lore, I know only that all of the sagas end in a great battle, with glorious deaths followed by an after-life in Valhalla. But glorious or otherwise, death is death. This will make a good series of conversations with John, Father, and Uncle Arch.

December 25. Christmas is cold. There is frost on the windows and snow on the ground. This is definitely not New Orleans. We went to Mass last night. John took me to a Catholic church, and, of course, the mass was the same Latin as in New Orleans, but the German prayers and the homily seemed directed almost as much to Herr Hitler as to God. Is this what Uncle Arch means when he talks about demagogues? Maybe here, though, it is *demigod* instead, although sometimes I'm not so sure about the *demi* part.

Nice letter from Mother and Father. Of course, this trip and my leather flying coat are my Christmas presents, so no parcel. Uncle Arch tells me he has a new pocketknife for me as a Christmas gift but didn't want to send it through the mail. I can have it when I return. Aunt Julie sent a parcel. Inside were some tarts and preserves. The tarts were a little dry until John soaked a cotton dishcloth in some whiskey, placed it on a tray of tarts, and put the tray in the oven for a few minutes. Then, they were EXCELLENT! Makes me miss home and the puddings, cakes, and pies of the season. Guess I'll miss Mardi Gras this year too and a big, good ol' purple, green, and gold king cake. Oh well, next year is the big year. I'll get to escort one of the princesses in the krewe's court.

John's letter from Uncle Arch says he agrees that John should come home, perhaps even sooner than March. John says we'll talk about it after New Year's. I forgot. We may be at war next year; maybe there won't be a Mardi Gras. I mean, how can you celebrate if you are at war?

Christmas is supposed to be a time of good cheer, and there seems to be a great deal of what we New Orleans people call bonhomie here, but it's more like mahogany veneer on poplar furniture. It looks expensive, but it really isn't, and it won't stand up to even regular wear and tear. The people seem cheerful in the restaurants and bars, but when they leave, a somberness overtakes them, and they walk the streets quietly. Still, there are daily marches of brown-shirted troopers through those same streets, and the marchers sing patriotic songs and shout slogans. Everyone cheers them, but when the parade passes on, the streets fall silent again and people are, once again, walking purposefully. Everyone has taken to greeting one another with "Heil Hitler" and giving the "Ave Caesar" salute of a raised and outstretched right arm. I found it amusing at first, almost as if they were role-playing in a children's game, but I'm beginning to think that this is what my history tutor, Monsieur Lattimer, calls "conformity of thought." He says such conformity led to historical events like the Inquisition in Spain. I think going home early might not be a bad idea. I enjoy learning German, but I have to say I can understand people who are different being afraid of this society. It is strange when you realize that Germany, as it is called now, has only existed for a little over a hundred years. It is not even as old as the United States. The Germany that Herr Hitler seems to want is even bigger than the Holy Roman Empire. But it is clear to me that Mr. Hitler does not consider himself the equivalent of Charlemagne or Pepin le Bref but instead of Nero or Caligula. He is a human God.

John has given me a comparison edition of *Mein Kampf*. That is, it has German on one page and the English translation on the facing page. He says he knows I won't like it but that I should read it anyway and that I should pay particular attention to the German words as well as the English. I can see I'll have a well thumbed German dictionary by the end of the book.

December 27. John's right; I don't like it. All Hitler does is blame other people. But I'll keep plowing through it. I hope John doesn't expect me to read *Das Kapital* in German as well.

January 3, 1939. New year. Very windy, and the snow is a dirty color, adding even more to the depressing atmosphere. John and I have decided to go home at the end of the month. He says we'll go by train and spend a few days in Paris to enliven us. Then we'll catch a ship at Cherbourg. That will be a faster crossing, and we'll take a Cunard or French vessel. No more German *Sieg Heil*-ing at meals and overly superior stewards who snicker when you crumble bread into your hot soup.

January 13. Today a funny thing happened. Funny strange, not funny ha. In the midmorning, we went to a café on Uhland Street, not far from the zoo. While I was trying to listen for words I could recognize during John's conversation with a man he introduced as Herr Linden, I noticed a man and a woman at another table paying close attention to the conversation. It was like they were both trying to listen but didn't want to appear curious. I was seated at the corner of the table leaning back in my chair, and they were directly in my line of vision. I could look over their heads, or through them, for that matter, and see them without appearing to stare. The man wore a dark-brown leather overcoat, the woman a knee-length black leather coat. The man had a slouch hat on the table, and the woman wore a beret. Not a French beret but a larger variety, almost a Tam o' Shanter, although it lacked the pom-pom on the top. It, too, was black, giving her an overall sepulchre-like appearance, contrasted only by the red lipstick she was wearing. When Herr Linden left the café, the woman followed him out the door. The man waited for us to leave, and I saw him get into a taxi behind the one we took back to John's apartment.

John, who had been seated with his back to the two, looked worried when I told him about them in the taxi. He thanked me and told me to keep my eyes out for either of the two in the coming days. He left the apartment and didn't come back until after midnight.

January 15. I met another group of Hitler Youth today at a New Year's reception the American Embassy gave for American citizens. Like Ernst, from the youth-movement meeting, they were from families that had lived in the United States and then returned to Germany. Some have been back here as long as four years. Others are newcomers, but all of them speak German and wore their uniforms. They were very proud. They were also what Father would describe as insufferable, with their Hitler this and Hitler that. Several of the boys said they want to join the Party when they are eligible, just as Ernst had said when I spoke with him. One boy, Peter Heinz, told me he will join the army to "defend the Fatherland." He said that if he joined now he thought he would gain rank quickly since, as he declared, "there is to be a war, and lots of soldiers will be coming in below me." If Uncle Arch were here, I imagine he would be describing these boys like kkk members. Certainly, they strut around like kkkers on parade, what with their banners and slogans and songs. They're definitely not the Boy Scouts, but from what little I know, I think they are scarier even than the kkk.

I think the American ambassador was embarrassed when all these Nazi Americans turned up. He left the reception early, and it was his reception. Here's what I find strange—all these families have "come back" to Germany, but none of them seem to have yet given up their American citizenship.

January 31. Crossed the border between Germany and France last night. The train ride was a long one, and after an initial attempt at conversation, John and I rode in silence. He seemed occupied in his thoughts, and all I could think about were the what-ifs of getting across the border and out of what has become a depressing episode in my life. I do not understand this seemingly blind allegiance to a short man with a loud voice and a very bad haircut and mustache.

It seemed to take forever to get through the German emigration station. According to John, they used to just come on the train, check passports, and ask you if you were carrying any large sums of money. But now, you must disembark and have your luggage searched by these dark-gray-coated German inspectors who wear the bright-red, white, and black Nazi armbands. The officers wear high-crowned hats, and the sergeants have short shakos. Both prominently mount the art deco–stylized Nazi Eagle above the cap bill.

John says they're looking for Jews trying to cross the border with money and personal goods. This is a very strange world, in this new year of 1939; there are American Germans coming back to Germany and German Jews trying to get out.

John showed the emigration guards an identity card he received from the American Consul in Berlin giving him official diplomatic courier status. He is carrying a pouch to the embassy in Paris. Still, we had to stand and wait on the platform in the cold. I hope these armbands are the last swastikas I see for a long time.

February 3, Paris. I don't know which is worse: being in a city in which the gaiety is forced and everyone knows a war is coming or being in a city in which the gaiety is real and no one seems to care that a war is coming. That's not from me; that's from John. Paris is all lights; the cafés and nightclubs along the Champs Élysées are full. People wear coats of blue and red, green, and olive brown. There is very little black to be seen. John says they are fools, but Premier Daladier has promised them no war, and they believe him.

We are staying on the Left Bank in a small hotel on the Rue de Babylone. John stays here when he is in Paris. In truth, it is very nice and comfortable. We have a suite with two bedrooms on the top floor, and I like the small cafés near at hand. They have excellent brioche and croissants, although I miss the sweeter beignets of New Orleans and the coffee isn't nearly strong enough. I've taken to asking for a double espresso and a pot of hot water, and then I make my own café Americano. I can also ask for a coffee press, although the espresso and hot water is faster.

The terrace of our suite looks out over the roofs of surrounding buildings up toward the Seine. It is nice, except the roofs have chimney pots and the smoke can be very bad, especially in the morning. Burning coal is not a pleasant smell. Still, why would one want to be out on the terrace in weather this cold and drizzly?

John has had appointments both days with someone from the embassy and with some other people he just refers to as "other people." He left me on my own because, after all, this is Paris, and I feel at home here. Monsieur Toussaint would be proud of my accent. When I wear the appropriate clothes, they take me as one of their own. I am also surprised at my Italian. Uncle Arch must be a very good teacher, because yesterday I was at a used bookstall looking for an original copy of *Tintin au pays des Soviets* (*Tintin in the Land of the Soviets*) for my collection of Tintin books when an Italian girl, who couldn't speak French, asked the bookseller if he had any back copies of *La Moda Illustrata*. When the bookseller didn't understand, I translated for her. He did not have any copies, and after I explained, the girl coyly suggested we might have "*una tazza di caffè*." She giggled as if she was being very forward, which, of course, she was. I suppose she was somewhere in her early twenties; she had dark, short hair and bright, golden-brown eyes. She was short but not too short, and her figure was slim but not too slim; I mean she had curves in the right places. I was tempted to tell her "No, thank you," but at the same time, I really wanted to see how far I could go with what appeared to be some mistaken situational awareness on her part, so I accepted. We walked to a small café off the boulevard, and I ordered croissants and coffee for the two of us. Her name was Gemma Sangiovanni, and she's from Rome. She has a little English but no French, having just arrived in Paris to begin training in one of the high-fashion houses here. The school the design house runs will teach her French as well as drawing, sewing, and, she hopes, modeling.

Her father is a businessman in Rome, buying and selling commodities of some sort. Or at least I think she said commodities. I had to ask her to repeat herself a few times, and once I blurted out, "*Lentemente, prego.*" (Slowly, please.) But I understood most of the conversation.

She told me how much she wanted to be in Paris. I asked her about Mussolini and things in Italy, but she passed off the entire subject, shrugging and waving the back of her hand while saying, *"Almeno i treni in orario."* (At least the trains run on time.)

I told her I was on my way back from Germany to the United States, and she sighed and wondered if she would ever get to New York. That, of course, is where she really wants to go, but her father cannot afford it. I told her that I wasn't going to New York either but to New Orleans by way of Baltimore and Washington, DC.

We were having a good time when she suggested I might like to join her and some of her friends that evening. She said her friends knew where the good bands were playing the hottest jazz, and it didn't cost much. She ended by asking if I perhaps had a cigarette.

I apologized, saying I did not smoke, and then I delivered the bad news: *"Io sono solo sedici anni."* (I'm only sixteen years old.) Well, you would have thought I had taken out a pistol and shot her. She fell back in her chair, her hand to her chest, and then covered her mouth. Then she laughed, a really loud belly laugh. Everyone in the café turned to look at us. Some of the people in the back actually stood up to see better.

Gemma leaned back in her chair a little and said, "Ma che sopresa!" (What a surprise!) Then, leaning forward with her elbows on the table, she said, "Ma sei così alto e virile!" (But you are so tall and manly!) After a moment, she rose from her chair, leaned over and took my chin in her hand, and kissed me on my cheek, whispering, "*Che peccato.*" (What a pity.) Then, finally, she said, "*Addio, bello*" (Good-bye, handsome) and was gone.

I haven't washed my face. The lipstick is still there. Last night I tried to sleep on my back so it wouldn't wipe off on the sheets. John laughed when I told him about the encounter, but then he sat me down with this serious face and warned me not to take myself too seriously or to play the role too well. There are, he said, women who might just take advantage of me.

I didn't tell him that I might actually like being taken advantage of, but...oh well. He has promised not to tell Mother and Father. Still, if you look just right in the mirror you can see the outline of her lips even now.

I will, of course, tell Uncle Arch.

February 6. Although I have haunted the bookstalls, I have not seen Miss Gemma again. I have, though, found a copy of the Tintin book I was searching for. It isn't as funny as I thought it should be, but anything is better than *Mein Kampf.* I have heard quite a bit of German in the bookstalls, with refugees attempting to sell first editions or second editions of this and that. John tells me it is the same on the streets where the antique shops are. Refugees offering to sell family heirlooms for the price of a ticket out of France to America or South America. It has been going on, John says, since 1933 but now there are Austrians, Czechs, and even a few Slovaks joining the crowds trying to get out of Europe. The price of antiques has fallen dramatically with the glut of small furniture that has come to the markets of Paris, Marseilles, and Cherbourg. Some luckier Germans have been able to sell their goods directly to Americans and Englishmen looking for bargains, and in the process, some have gained sponsors for immigration.

John says Paris is chock-full of Jewish writers, actors, film directors, and such who are all trying to get to England, Canada, or the United States. He has tried to talk with several of them about conditions in German cities other than Berlin, but they are too preoccupied with wanting to escape to speak at any length. John is especially interested in the number of arrests, but the only story the refugees tell is that they were afraid of being arrested themselves so they fled. They remain afraid, they tell John, of the German secret police—the Gestapo, they are called—because there are stories that other refugees have disappeared from Marseilles, Lyon, and even Paris. These are, John says, unsubstantiated reports as of yet. No one has yet come forward with absolute proof that people are being kidnapped by the Gestapo and taken back to Germany to concentration camps. No one knows for sure, and no one is willing to speak of any details they may know for fear of becoming a Gestapo target. I'm not supposed to know this, but many of the refugees are being sent to Marseilles, and some are being smuggled into British Palestine. Others are trying to get there on their own, but open travel is prohibited for refugees, and the British are trying hard to keep them out of Palestine.

John says his friends at the American, Canadian, and British embassies are inundated with requests for visas of any kind to get out of France. And just yesterday, John said, the embassy in Paris received notification that Thomas Mann had requested a visa to the United States from the US consul in Zurich. Think of that: a Nobel Prize–winning author is fleeing the Nazis. I'll ask Uncle Arch what he and Mr. Faulkner think of Mann, since I have yet to read his work. Perhaps I should buy one of his books to take on the ship with me. I could have John help me with the German. I wonder if *The Magic Mountain* might be too ambitious. Perhaps I can find a comparison copy in French and German at one of the bookstalls. I should have thought of this before we left Germany, but then, I didn't know Mr. Mann was going to be fleeing the Nazis, did I? Still, from what I've heard, Mann's works almost universally end with death, and I wonder if that's what I want right now? To read a book, no matter how well crafted, that speaks to death? No, maybe not at this time. There's going to be too much death, and I don't need to start dealing with it now. I'm sure the New Orleans public library has a translation, or maybe Tulane University; if not, I can order the book from New York or Chicago.

February 8. We took an overnight train from Paris to Cherbourg. Came aboard the ship at noon today. Small stateroom after so large a suite at the hotel. You know, I hadn't thought about it before, but we were staying on the Rue de Babylone, and this year the new Krewe of Babylon will have its first parade in Mardi Gras. Must be a message from the gods somewhere in there, but I'll be danged if I can figure it out. Anyway, if everything is on time, I'll get a couple of days of Mardi Gras. Some doubloons and king cake and real gaiety with no thought of what's to come after, except, of course, Lent.

Confession and Lent—but then there's always Easter and baseball to look forward to. We'll play baseball even during Lent.

February 9. The ship is full. There are so many people about that it is difficult to walk on deck. It's more like being on the midway at a carnival. There's no mindless strolling here, or you'll step on someone's heels. The weather is clear but cold. The sea is fine. I understand from the stewards that second and third class are full as well and that steerage is almost standing-room only. The steward says the ship's doctor hopes there is no outbreak of a contagious disease, because it would spread faster than old maids can spread a rumor, and in New Orleans that's plenty fast. He's particularly worried because there are lots of children in steerage. I stay inside reading all the magazines from the ship's library, which just happens to have a copy of *The Magic Mountain*. I'm still working on the last few pages of *Mein Kampf* (couldn't bear to do it while in cheerful Paris), so I'll give *The Magic Mountain* a pass. Strangely enough, John asked me if I had seen either the man or the woman from the coffee shop in Berlin. A couple of times he has had me bundle up in a deck chair while he makes the rounds of the deck. Other times I'm supposed to follow him at a fifty-foot interval. I'm supposed to watch for anyone taking an interest in him, especially if he stops to talk to someone. I think John is more than just a language student.

John, like a goodly number of other passengers, visits the wireless room several times a day to look at the wireless summaries of the news reports. He also listens to the radio in the lounge, but he must listen to the channel the ship's steward chooses, and they mostly have the BBC on. There are more than a few Germans on the ship, and a few French, but mostly British and several American families. Almost all of the Americans are from somewhere up north like New York, which is a little strange since our ship is bound for Baltimore. John says steerage is full of Eastern Europeans bound for the United States.

February 16. US immigration was much easier than Germany. There is a line for US citizens, and we got through very quickly. Once again, John had a consular courier pass. He had another courier bag he was going to drop at the State Department in Washington. I just changed trains in Washington. John stayed on for "some meetings," as he said. I wonder what kind of meetings. He said he'll be along in a couple of days but not 'til after Mardi Gras.

February 18. Home. My own bed felt soooo good last night. Finished *Mein Kampf* on train. Didn't like it, but I see the singleness of purpose Hitler has. Talk in the club car wasn't about Hitler, though. Some businessmen were saying a lot of things about rubber being so expensive and about the Japanese in Indochina. Gave the copy of *Wendermarke* to John to give to Uncle Arch. He can send it up to Mr. Faulkner as a late Christmas gift.

CHAPTER 20

PARCEL FOR FAULKNER

LITTLE ARCH MAKES THE STOP in Oxford on a flight to
Helena, Arkansas, where he is to meet with some small landowners about buying timber rights. It is a little out of the
way, but he has a message to deliver to Mr. Faulkner that the
Judge didn't want to put in writing. He also carries the copy
of *Wendermarke* wrapped in brown butcher paper.

It is the first time he has been to the Oxford airport, and
as with most places, except for Memphis and New Orleans,
the locals are surprised when an extremely large Negro climbs
out of the cockpit of an expensive Stinson SR-8 aircraft. Since
he doesn't need fuel to make the onward trip to Helena, Little
Arch doesn't have to deal with any of the locals except to find
a ride to Rowan Oak, which is the name of Faulkner's house.
He does this by overpaying a man who has an old Ford two-
door and who is a grease-and-rag man at the airport. That is,
he cleans and refuels airplanes, of which there aren't many on
a given day. He is happy to make the three dollars Little Arch

offers him for the round-trip and doesn't care that Little Arch is a Negro.

But on the way from the airfield, for that is what it is—a grass strip not unlike the one the Judge has in the meadow behind his barn—the driver tries to pump Little Arch for information. He figures he can trade the information later for some corn liquor. Everybody always wants to know about foreigners, as people from outside Oxford and the university are known. Little Arch sees no reason not to be truthful. He is delivering a package from Judge Cameron to William Faulkner. The package contains a book. He will be returning shortly to the airfield and continuing his trip to Helena, Arkansas, where he will be buying, he hopes, some timber rights.

Little Arch can tell his driver is disappointed that the news isn't something more nefarious. Perhaps he was expecting some kind of conspiracy, because Oxford has never before seen a six-foot-four Negro arrive in a ten-thousand-dollar airplane. Perhaps Little Arch is really a eunuch advisor to some sheik of Araby who wants Faulkner to write his memoirs. But if he is, wouldn't he have a funny accent? This boy, the driver thinks, sounds like somebody from Mississippi, although he pronounces all of his words clearly and doesn't use the slang of the local Negroes. Well, he can make up whatever story he wants, because no one else is going to speak with the Negro before he leaves, except, of course, Faulkner, and Faulkner doesn't have much truck with any of the white trash hereabouts. Yep, he can pretty well make up whatever story he wants. The driver settles back in the seat to wait on the return of the light-skinned Negro, who is making his way up the cypress-lined pea-gravel walkway to the front of the house. He does wonder why the boy is going to the front door. Negros should go to the kitchen door.

A dark-haired lady wearing a floral-print dress answers the door. She is surprised at the size of the man filling the door-way and that he is a Negro. Her initial response is fear, and it shows as she thrusts her right hand up to cover her mouth. Little Arch apologizes for startling her, and then says he has a package from Judge Cameron for Mr. Faulkner. The lady cannot, or will not, invite him into the house, for someone might be looking. Instead, she tells him to wait on the porch and she will find "Bill." She corrects herself quickly, saying, "I mean, Mr. Faulkner." This short exchange takes place through the screen door, but when she steps away into the house, she turns back and closes the hardwood door, locking it and then asking herself if the screen door is locked.

This does not upset Little Arch in the least. He is used to people being afraid of him. Some are afraid because he is big, some because he is black, and some because he is big and black. Well, he's not actually black—his skin is such that if he wore a hat, he could pass as a Hispanic or someone from the South Sea Islands. Still, in the Deep South—and Oxford, Mississippi, is pretty deep in that Deep South—Hispanics and South Sea islanders are treated the same as the Negroes.

After a few moments, the door opens again; Faulkner stands behind the screen door trying to remember where he had met this large person. From Little Arch's perspective, there stands before him a little man in baggy khaki trousers and a blue work shirt worn under a canvas blazer. He is shod in scuffed brown brogans and carries a straight briar pipe. His eyes are reddish and a little watery, as though he has a cold, but the smell of alcohol seems to belie that theory.

"Mr. Faulkner, I'm Joshua Weems. We met at Judge Cameron's house down south of here last October."

It takes Faulkner only a moment, but he opens the screen door and advances out onto the porch. He offers his hand, and Joshua swallows it with his own. He then holds out the butcher-paper parcel.

"It's from the Judge. It's a copy of your novel *Pylon* in German. His nephew Shelby Devereux picked it up in Germany for you. The Judge also wanted me to tell you that what he feared most would probably happen by the end of the year and that you should invest your money in Boeing, Lockheed Aircraft, and the new shipyard the Ingalls Company is building in Pascagoula."

Faulkner looks a little dazed. "What is coming? What is it he feared most? Please remind me." Perhaps Faulkner had been napping. The image passes through Little Arch's mind as an appropriate metaphor for the nation, and so he can see a bleary, red-eyed Uncle Sam just roused from a nap asking, "What is coming? What is it he feared most?" Little Arch smiles slightly at the thought of the simile and then answers.

"War, Mr. Faulkner, war is coming. The Judge says that by the end of the year all of Europe will be at war, and England and others will turn to us for help. He suggests you invest your money in the companies that make airplanes for the army and ships for the navy."

Faulkner musters an "Oh" and then another "Oh." Then he manages a "Thank you" and finally, a "Please tell the Judge thank you."

Realizing further conversation will be stilted and of little use, Little Arch excuses himself by noting he has to return to the airport for he has business in Arkansas and the day is getting on. As the big man turns away toward the gravel walk, he hears Faulkner mutter to himself, "Money? What money?"

CHAPTER 21

PLOT AND COUNTERPLOT

LITTLE ARCH RETURNS FROM HIS Arkansas trip with the cutting rights to more than two thousand acres of prime timber. He and the Judge sit for many hours forming plans for when they will cut the various stands of pine, hickory, oak, and poplar.

"Some of the stands have time-limitation contracts requiring we cut the timber within eighteen months. I assume you tried for longer periods?" the Judge asks, already knowing the answer. Joshua would have asked for a three-year period, but one seldom obtained a contract for that long in the timber business.

Taking up a pen with red ink, the Judge marks these holdings on the map. "We'll have to cut these first then. If they're pulp pine, we'll just take the loads to the nearest paper mills, but if they're white pine or hardwood trees we'll have to take our saw machines up and mill it and then throw up some sheds to dry and store the lumber. I anticipate that with the coming of war, the prices for lumber, along with everything else, will rise significantly. The sheds should be on the property fairly near where the trees are milled into lumber so that the transportation costs are negligible." Here he begins checking Joshua's list, looking for the fields that are pulp and those that are not.

"This means more trips to Arkansas to arrange to rent some sheds and lease property on which we can build others. With our timber rights in Alabama, Louisiana, Mississippi, and Tennessee, we're beginning to move into the big time of the timber business in the South. That most of these timber rights are on property owned by Negroes makes us just a little unusual." The Judge stands up from the desk and stretches his arms above his head.

"That will also give me the opportunity to meet with these landowners and explain our views about how the war will drive up prices, and, if they can, the farmers should store as much of what they are growing instead of selling it immediately. Remind me, please, that we want to consider offering a small percentage of any profit we make on government lumber sales as an added incentive for any further purchase of timber rights.

"Of course, the government will eventually bring in price controls, so our early-on larger profits will not be available later in the conflict, but here, at the beginning, those who have large stocks of commodities will make more than a little money."

"Now that," Joshua exclaims, "is exactly the type of advice that will convince more and more of these smaller farmers to follow the lead you've begun here in Mississippi."

The Judge is tired; he spent most of the previous night out with the sheriff. He pours himself a brandy and flops into one of the leather chairs across his office from the desk. He rolls the brandy glass in his hands, motioning for Joshua to take up residence in the other chair.

The Judge begins to speak. "Things are better, and after last night, I think they will get a little better still. I'm going to share this with you, but it can go no further than the door of this office. Shelby, and especially Miss Julia, should not know of it." He gestures at the closed office door with the brandy glass as he speaks.

"For the foreseeable future, Banker Thompson and the local klan will continue to be thorns in our collective side as they try to undo our grange. The klan rank and file seem not to understand that their actions only aid the banks and large-farm owners in taking over the farms of the small landowners, white and black. With a fire here, a broken dam there, or maybe just a poisoned mule, they continue to dig away at our foundations. The sheriff has a difficult time breaking through the protective wall of silence the klan has built around its members." He stops long enough to enjoy the bouquet of the brandy and then continues.

"Sometimes Cleveland catches the perpetrators of the crime, but more often than not, they escape justice. That may change, though, since we caught Jasper Donald last night trying to set fire to the barn on the Peebles' place down near the county line. It was pure happenstance, but Cleveland and I were coming back from the courthouse at about eight o'clock and became suspicious when we saw Donald's pickup parked behind the Cities Service gas station. Donald was hoisting two five-gallon cans of gas into the bed. That the station was closed added to our suspicion, and ten gallons of gasoline is a lot to be carrying around in the bed of your truck when you don't own any farm machinery. So, we switched to Cleveland's personal vehicle and spent the evening following Donald.

"You remember Donald lost his farm to the bank last year and came to town to do whatever work he could. His son is in the CCC in one of the camps in Tennessee. His wife works as a cook for the Majors family over on the Hattiesburg road, where she is responsible for feeding the hired help their lunches. Donald, though, works for the Wilsons at the sawmill over by Homestead. He operates the machine that cuts stove wood." The Judge is referring to the ten-inch billets of wood that many people use in their wood-burning cook- and heating stoves.

Joshua nods slightly and adds, "He makes some extra money driving a truck to deliver the wood to the farms that can afford to buy it from the sawmill. I think he actually delivers the stove wood Miss Julia uses."

The Judge drags a footstool over with the toe of his boot and places his left leg upon it. He often gets a stiff knee from the very small piece of shrapnel that lodged itself behind his left kneecap. The doctors offered to try to take it out but could not assure him that the result might not leave him with a permanently stiff leg, so he chose the infrequent discomfort that results from the steel fragment becoming hung up between the bottom of his femur and his kneecap. It will move in a few minutes, but for now he will just rest it awhile. He continues talking about Donald, and Joshua knows that he is being given a background brief and that the Judge will reach the crux of the matter sooner or later.

"Like us, the Donald family were latecomers to this area. Whereas we joined family here in the county, the Donalds are part of that infamous group we Southerners like to refer to as carpetbaggers. They arrived from the North with their possessions in carpet suitcases and proceeded to buy, for pennies on the dollar, land that had been taken by the Reconstruction governments for unpaid taxes."

"Like your granddaddy's place in Alabama," Joshua interjects.

"Yes, just like our granddaddy's place. Don't forget that he was your granddaddy as much as mine. And don't forget that your daddy was born a free man and that your grandmother was a slave in name only and was actually a free woman when your daddy was born.

"Well, there are actually more than a few of those families in the county, and even now, in 1939, the stigma still clings, although they have been farming the land or at least living in the towns for almost seventy years. Their efforts to fit in are rewarded by being left alone for the most part, but no original settler wants his daughter to marry into a family of carpetbaggers. Nor are the sometimes beautiful daughters of these families to be courted by even the basest of first families' sons. Donald's family came from Pennsylvania. We have others who came from Maryland, Ohio, Illinois, Tennessee, and elsewhere to cash in on the land bargains that Reconstruction provided.

It was almost as if the Mississippi Territory had been reopened for settlement as it had originally back in 1803 or so.

"Many of the families that were dispossessed by Reconstruction governments pulled up stakes and moved to Texas and the Oklahoma Territory, where land was still available for homestead. Others gathered together in extended family groups, scraped together what little cash they could, and bought much smaller parcels of land than those farms they lost. Generally, the land wasn't as fertile as the bottomland of their first farms, which now lay in the grasp of the latecomers. The soil was rather more red clay than the black-earth alluvial soil they once possessed, but it was still in Mississippi. I know you know all of this, but sometimes it helps to remember the perspective from which we're going to consider something.

"There remains deep-seated anger and mistrust underlying our patchwork society. Everybody thinks we just hate Yankees, but in many ways, we hate ourselves—or at least people who should be considered ourselves. But slavery, the war, Reconstruction, and the Depression are proving hard things to overcome. Few travelers to the South see the divisions that exist within our own society, preferring to think us a monolithic block of rural crackers—all of whom need to be punished for the pernicious leavings of slavery. In fact, though, there are many rifts and divisions within our own culture caused by history, religion, and economics. The descendants of the original settlers don't like the latecomers, all of whom are, in their eyes, carpetbaggers. The Baptists don't like the Catholics or Jews and aren't all that friendly with the Methodists or Presbyterians.

The Catholics keep to themselves too much, as do the Jews. The Methodists and the Presbyterians like everybody, but it doesn't seem to do much good. The poor don't like the rich, so that means 'most everybody dislikes the Episcopalians, except, of course, when a Baptist family gets money and some of them become Episcopalians." He smiles at the last observation. It isn't necessarily true all the time, but it is true enough some of the time that people can poke fun at it.

"The South is just like everywhere else, but somehow slavery and the rebellion make us all suspect. You know there are klan organizations in Michigan and Ohio that rival the size of those we have down here. You're too young to remember this, but fifteen years ago, candidates for local, state, and national office across the country ran on the klan ticket. There were klownsmen being elected mayor, alderman, and state representative in Maine, Oregon, and a host of other states in between. Even today, there are members of both houses of the US Congress who are members of the klan. With the Depression and the growth of Roosevelt's New Deal, the klan as a political force has fallen off, and now it's more of an underground movement led by those who believe themselves dispossessed by Reconstruction, who seek to avenge wrongs both real and imagined. As with any other grievance, these crimes of dispossession and wrongful treatment grow with each telling. Those who define themselves as avengers of wrongs have been joined by the pretenders, the latecomers who find that joining the klan is one way they're allowed to be equals and move into the closed society of the first families. They sit and plot together.

Of course, there are those who join simply because they are haters and bigots. Every society has some of those.

"Sometimes, when I give thought to the matter, I wish the klan was more like the dispossessed Russian aristocracy that haunt the salons and restaurants of Paris and other European cities. There, like here, it simply will not do that their scions or daughters mingle with the hoi polloi of Europe, even though many of them are reduced in fortune to being waiters, maître d's, or clerks. They are still princes and princesses, dukes and duchesses, barons and baronesses, counts and countesses, and winners of this royal medal or that. So, they keep to their own and create secret organizations to plot the overthrow of the communists and return themselves to power. They populate small, working-class hotels and cafés, mostly in Paris and London, using—when they can—their past glories, real and imagined, to seek entrance into the salons of the wealthy, on whom many depend upon indulgences in return for ennobling dinner parties and other fêtes as Russian royalty.

"It amuses me to think of all the plotting that goes on in many of the cafés in Paris. Big words, grand ideas, division of the spoils...In truth, though, it is plotting without action, for the plots are mostly fantasies dreamed up under the influence and induced bravery of cheap cognac. Dreams that swirl in the god-awful Gauloise smoke of the cafés and dissipate when the doors are opened. But the smell lingers in the hair and clothes of the dreamers. That's the mark of a Russian plotting revolution in Paris. He smells of Gauloises and cheap cognac."

The Judge sips at the brandy, thinking it much better than the cognac and vodka those dispossessed Russians would gulp down as they excitedly debated who of them would become the prime minister and who the defense minister and, of course, who and where were the closest relatives of the late Tsar Nicolas.

Looking at Joshua through the glass, he continues. "Not so the dreams of the secret organizations that plot to gain and hold power in the South. The plots they plant bear bitter fruit. They are more like Mussolini's Blackshirts or the Nazi Brownshirts, who have captured power by eliminating those who rose to challenge them; and they did so through violence. They preach hate. I know the only thing keeping an American Fascist Party from congealing is the lack of a charismatic leader who can crystallize the disparate state organizations. As it is, the leader of each individual statewide klan organization thinks he is uniquely qualified to head the effort, and as a result, the klan as a national institution remains divided by ego. We have to keep it so, for if we fail, then the United States faces the same fate as Europe. And thus, young Joshua, we have to do our part."

He rises from the chair and bends his knees. The shrapnel has moved a little, and he can now get up and down without significant pain.

"So, to help do our part, last night we recruited Mr. Donald to our cause. He isn't what one might call a willing recruit, but with the threat of a minimum five-year prison sentence hanging over his head...Well, let's just say that while he may be unenthusiastic, he will be most useful. He is a wrecking-crew leader, so he is involved in planning and executing the nefarious activities our local klownsmen may be contemplating.

"I don't think we'll ever be able to bring a legal case against the klan, but perhaps we can weaken it from the inside out. My ultimate goal is to interfere enough so that we sow the seeds of suspicion. They will know there are spies in their midst, but they will not know who the spies are and that suspicion will cause internal rifts. We'll never be able to bring down the Banker Thompsons of the world, but if we attack at the weakest points—which are people like Donald—we can lessen the support for the klan and its activities. It isn't enough just to know what they're going to do; we have to take action to prevent them from doing it and, in doing so, suggest the names of people who cannot be trusted. That is, when we stop some action, we'll let it be known through certain channels that one of the Gilberts might have said something about what was going to happen. Now, of course, the Gilberts are hardcore klan and would never let something slip, but we'll eventually make them pariahs if we do our job right. Never underestimate the power of a good rumor, especially if you keep feeding the maw of schadenfreude with a tidbit here and a tidbit there. The key, of course, is to develop a number of low-level sources within the local klavern—and we've started that with Donald. We'll have the kleagles chasing imaginary agents within their ranks through our misdirection program. We may even be able to sow enough discord and mistrust to shut down many of their activities, especially if they think they're being betrayed from the top down."

"And you want me to drop some comments in various places throughout the Negro community. Is that it?" Joshua's grin goes from ear to ear.

"Well, certainly, as I said, never underestimate the power of a good rumor. Perhaps we should start with Mr. Frank Gilbert's trip to New York. Now, I happen to know he went up there to see a doctor, but let's tell people that was just a cover story and he actually went up North to talk to some Yankee bankers about arranging some loans because the local bank's interest rates are too high. Something like…Mr. Gilbert is going to bring Yankee money into Mississippi, but the bankers up there are afraid of the klan, so Mr. Gilbert has agreed to do something about getting the klan under control if the Yankee bankers will give him a good rate."

"My, my! Are you trying to get old man Gilbert hung from a tree?" Joshua tries hard to swallow the guffaw that traps itself in his throat as he asks the question. "Ain't nobody wants Yankee money down here, klan or otherwise."

"Well, it's the kind of rumor that will hang on for a long while. Whatever Gilbert tries to do, people are going to think it has something to do with his 'agreement' with the Yankee bankers. It'll slow him up a bit and maybe create a little distrust between him and Banker Thompson. With Gilbert slowed up, and with a wrecking-crew leader under our control, we can be more aggressive at stopping the klan's activities in the county. Our next step is to get Donald to share details about other members of the klan's midlevel echelons and then to come up with a plan for selectively turning one against another."

"Sort of like the 'great game' of England versus Russia, only with people in a county instead of countries in a region," Little Arch is intrigued, and he laughs to himself as he realizes that he is intrigued by intrigue.

"Exactly. And like the 'great game,' it is more a chess match than a football game. It will take years to play out, and I'm not sure we have years before the board upon which we play our game isn't dramatically transformed. We shall see."

CHAPTER 22

SHELBY MATRICULATES AT LOYOLA

"ARE YOU GOING TO PLAY sports?" Shelby's mother's question isn't about sports, though; it's about his intentions. She has her suspicions.

"Yes, ma'am. I thought I might fence in the winter term, and maybe I'll consider some tennis in the spring, but we'll see."

"What? Not baseball? You love baseball."

"Yes, ma'am, I do, but baseball requires a time commitment I can't make right now. Maybe next year." He doesn't seem defensive, she thinks, but then he continues.

"Besides, I want to do as much flying as possible. There's a war coming, and I want to make sure I can get into the air corps. The more flying hours I have, the more likely I'll be able to just enter the corps directly without having to go through cadet training. Now that Uncle Arch has taught me aerobatics, I want to become a certified instructor, and that takes five hundred hours of flying time." He makes the comment offhandedly, as if it is no more important than what math course he'll take first semester.

"But if there is a war, you'll stay in college until you finish your degree, and then maybe you can join up." His mother is having none of this "rushing off to war" talk. Besides, Roosevelt promised to keep American boys from fighting in a European war. She trusts Roosevelt, even if he is a Protestant; after all, her very own brother is an Episcopalian.

This tension around Shelby's possible role in an upcoming war has been growing over the past few weeks, and Shelby wants none of the escalating drama that accompanies talk of his joining the army or naval air arms. His mother is dead set against it; his father attempts to mediate but finds himself more on the side of his wife than on that of his only son.

"Yes, ma'am." Shelby short-circuits his mother's distress by acquiescing. There is absolutely no need for crying today, and he knows that if he pushes his position, his mother will cry. Perhaps he should live in a dorm rather than at home. He would see his mother less and thus be less likely to upset her, especially when he leaves the house with his flying coat, boots, and helmet. I guess I could just keep my gear in the car, he thinks. His solution satisfies him, although he does take great pleasure in occasionally gazing at the helmet and coat hanging from the coatrack in his bedroom. He leaves the breakfast table to go to his orientation as part of the entering freshman class of Loyola University.

The welcoming ceremony is followed by a mass in the chapel and then a reception. Shelby knows many of the boys he is entering with, having encountered them in one context or another throughout his New Orleans life. Loyola is mostly a commuter school, with the majority of its students coming from the environs of New Orleans.

"It's on the radio. I heard it in my car. Germany has invaded Poland." This from a tall, sandy-haired boy over by the punch bowl. He towers over the others gathered around him. Shelby recognizes him as one of the new boys recruited from somewhere up north to play basketball and baseball for the school. Apparently, he turned down Notre Dame because it was too cold in Indiana.

"So, what are we supposed to do on Saturdays if there are no football games?"

"What?" Shelby is caught off guard by the question from one of his classmates.

"What do we do on Saturdays, since the college canceled the football program?" It's Alexander Shipman. Shelby knows him from church. They were both acolytes.

"Did they cancel the football team?" Shelby hadn't heard, but he's more interested in the sandy-haired boy's description of what he heard on the radio than he is in Alex's lament about football; still, he comments.

"We'll just go to the Tulane games. Their team has always been better than ours, and we get our dates from Sophie Newcomb anyway, so there won't be much of a change." Shelby isn't worried about what to do on Saturdays, because he knows he'll be flying, but now he also knows that his timeline has become much shorter.

"Germany in Poland. Will the French and English honor their pledge to defend Poland?" the sandy-haired Yankee asks Professor Jones, who immigrated from Wales to teach at Loyola.

"The only thing I've learned about pledges in the political world is that they cause a great deal of heartbreak. The First World War was fought because of political entanglements and the European royal families' jealousies. And now we have England and France ensuring Polish sovereignty. Yes, Mr. Stanley, I do believe England will stand behind her promises, but I fear that she is not the United Kingdom of the last century and that Germany is far more powerful than any of us think."

Shelby does not enter the conversation. He is not interested in the politics, for he has already chosen sides. He has seen the Germans and their "New Germany," and he wants no part of it. "And I'll bet the French and British don't either," he mumbles as he leaves the reception and heads to the airport. He has a lot of flying to do and very little time to do it. "Let's see. Tonight, it'll be Mobile and back. That should give me another five hours or so of night flying time to add to my pilot's log. On Saturday, I'll fly up to Mississippi to see Uncle Arch. I wonder what he'll say about my plan." Shelby, like many pilots who fly a lot of solo time, often talks to himself, and, as he heads for his car, he is once again reviewing aloud the letter he will leave for his mother and father.

CHAPTER 23

LOOK AWAY, DIXIELAND

April 1944, Sixty miles northwest of Paris

ONE…TWO…THREE SHORT FLASHES; ONE…TWO LONG flashes. The lights come from the far tree line alongside a small cleared field. "This is the spot," the pilot says aloud to himself, since he is the only one in the all-black Westland Lysander. The wind is behind him, so he flies over the small field just enough to turn on his wing and make a steep approach into the almost impossibly small opening in the otherwise wooded area. There is only the smallest sliver of a moon, so he relies heavily on his excellent night vision to see through the deep darkness—the darkness that both protects and threatens him.

He rolls out of the steep turn, puts the flaps into the 100 percent deployed position, and eases off his throttle. After what seems only a second, the aircraft bounces briefly as the wheels hit the ground. "Not too hard," the pilot says aloud. "No, in fact, given the circumstances, pretty damned good, I would say." Once he has stopped the agile aircraft, he nurses the throttle a little to the front and turns the high-wing airplane around. He bounces it over the uneven ground toward the tree line over which he passed when landing. The Resistance is good at what it does, and they have chosen the downwind side of the clearing so that, once loaded, he can simply take off without again having to taxi the length of the clearing.

As he approaches the tree line, he once again turns the aircraft so that its nose faces away from the trees and into the wind. He draws his pistol and waits for the aft cowling to be opened by someone on the ground. As the cowling is pulled back, he points his pistol and, yelling to be heard over the engine, says, *"Je voudrais être dans le pays du coton."*

And shouting back in what seems a familiar voice comes, *"Regardez loin, Dixieland!"*

He motions with the pistol for the person to mount into the seat behind him in the cockpit. Once the cowling closes, he does not wait but pushes the throttle all the way forward. His flaps are already full down. Halfway across the field, the Lysander begins to bounce, and three-quarters of the way across, her wheels lift. The pilot holds the stick as far back into his lap as he dares, his left hand holding the throttle full forward to keep it from slipping backward. The black bird begins to fly. It clears the trees at the edge of the field by no more than three feet, but as far as the pilot is concerned it is enough, for he has little intention of flying much higher on his way across France and the English Channel.

Twisting his body in the cockpit, he yells to his passenger, *"Utilisez le casque."*

"I already have the headset on," he hears in a voice now even more familiar.

"John, is that you?"

"Yes, Shelby. It is. But the question is, what on earth are you doing in an RAF Lysander in the middle of France tonight?"

"Really, Cousin? You think the question is what am *I* doing here when the real question is what are *you* doing here. I'm just on loan to the British Special Operations Element because they need some pilots who are fluent in French. So, they plucked some of us out of the Special Operations Squadron to stand in for some of their boys who are down with the flu. So, it's very natural *I'm* here, but what the hell are *you* doing being picked up outside Nazi-occupied Paris and supported by members of the French Resistance? I thought you had some sort of job with the Department of State making all the niceties work with the Free French and such. Didn't I hear you were with General de Gaulle somewhere?"

All the time Shelby is questioning John he is trimming up the Lysander—flaps up, throttle set at cruise, trim tabs neutral—and scanning the darkness for forms and things that should not be there. On these missions, he often prays for God to protect him from things that go bump in the night. It is just a habit, but he sees no harm in taking God on the flight with him.

He uses his penlight to read his magnetic compass since he has turned off all the cockpit lights. He turns to the heading that will be his route for the next twenty minutes. He is not making directly for the coast, because if someone has heard the aircraft in the clearing and reported it to the Germans, they will assume he is making directly for the coast and will take measures to intercept him. He, however, has no such intention; instead, he will fly north until he passes into Belgium and then will make for the coast north of Dunkirk. This will allow him to cross the Channel just above its narrowest point at Calais. There is an RAF base just across the Channel where he can refuel before heading on to his home air station at Tempsford.

"Better cinch yourself in tightly," he warns John. "It could be a little bumpy since we'll be flying at about twenty feet or so."

"Right you are, old chap." John attempts the best British accent he can, and as he does so, the aircraft hits a downdraft that sucks it even closer to the trees. John's stomach falls even further than the aircraft, but luckily he doesn't lose his dinner. There is, after all, no dinner to lose. For that matter, there is no lunch or even breakfast to lose, either. For the past twenty-four hours, he has been bundled here, trundled there, stuffed down in a barrel on a truck, curled into the trunk of a car, and— ignominy of ignominies—wedged in among a group of pigs in an animal cart. But now he is safely on his way out of France aboard an RAF aircraft. Safety has become a relative term in John Cameron's world, and for him, the back seat of a single-engine airplane flying just above the trees in the darkest part of the night while being hunted by German radar and night fighters is safer than a Paris café and its Gestapo informants.

His thoughts are broken by Shell in the front seat. "I sure wish we were in my Mosquito. I'd have you back in a tick.

These Lysanders will only make about 180. We could double that in a Mossy, but if we have to go down, these things are much more survivable than the plywood the Moss is made from." Shell chats away, but then he abruptly remembers that going down is not, in any way, a survivable situation for his passenger.

"Damn, John. I didn't mean we might be going down or anything like that. I have every reason to believe we'll make this flight out with nothing other than a few air pockets as hindrances." He swallows hard, hoping he has not upset John with the talk of having to put the aircraft down.

"No worries, old boy," John says, attempting his British accent again. "I know the drill. If, for any reason, we have to land or crash, you are to shoot me. That is, of course, if I'm not already dead from crunching this capsule between my teeth. Fear not; if we go down, I'll be dead before you get out of your seat. You won't have to shoot your old cousin."

Shell waves his gloved hand from the front seat as an acknowledgment and as a thank you to John for his comment—for he was absolutely correct. On penalty of court martial, Lysander special-duty pilots were under strict orders to shoot their passengers should they be forced to put their aircraft on the ground. Wasn't there something more pleasant they could discuss?

"Hey, what's with that stupid recognition signal, 'I wish I was in the land of cotton'? Where the hell did that come from? And 'Look away, Dixieland'?" Shell can hardly restrain himself from laughing.

John makes no such attempt and laughs into the microphone as he explains. "Well, we don't come up with those things, you know. They're written by…What do you Brits call them? Oh, yes—Boffins. They're written by Boffins back at SOE headquarters. Sometimes they have a bit of fun with us. They'll put in something a little personal that lightens moments that otherwise might be…well, you know. Sort of inside jokes and such. Would you like to do a chorus of Dixie in French?"

Shell laughs into his microphone and begins, "Oh, I wish I was…" but stops. "Hey, what is this 'you Brits' business?" But he doesn't continue, and silence fills the cockpit.

There are so many things they could discuss, but as on the night trip on the train from Germany in 1939, they are too occupied with thoughts of making a safe journey through a strange and dangerous land. Each sits in the cockpit thinking not of home but of things that must be done. John thinks of the next steps in his mission once he lands, but Shell's focus is more immediate, as his eyes seek shape and form in the gray-black night and his ears monitor the performance of his radial engine.

A shadow crosses the weak moonlight, causing Shell to quickly look upward. It's only a cloud, and ahead of them, there are more clouds, but even as they settle in, Shell continues to scan the sky above for night fighters and the roads below for traffic. He needs to avoid both. But there are no fighters and no traffic, and, after the correct amount of time, he banks the aircraft to the left. He rolls out on a westerly heading, and before long, he can discern the English Channel as a black line on the charcoal-gray horizon.

As they clear the French coast, a line of red tracers reaches out for the aircraft. A searchlight comes on and begins to sweep the air above the water; it is looking for them. The enemy has heard them, but based on where the tracers went, Shell determines they have not seen him. He pushes the aircraft down until it is just above the churning waves. The weather over the Channel is not good, and the sea is running heavy. The lower they go, the faster the searchlight's beam will fall behind them, since the horizon for the land-based light shrinks with their lower altitude. It's no problem, really, because Shell crosses the Channel all the time in his Mosquito, and the enemy seldom sees him unless, of course, there is a bright moon. But tonight, there is no "gunner's moon," and he and John will make the crossing in ten minutes.

As the Lysander approaches the coast, Shell flicks his radio switch. "Control—Snapper one two. Control—Snapper one two." He turns up his instrument lights so that he can read his fuel gauge and is surprised that he has enough gas to make his base at Tempsford. He will have no reserve when he lands, but the weather doesn't seem bad enough that he might have to try to go elsewhere, so he elects to keep going.

"Snapper one two—Control. Go ahead."

"Control—Snapper one two. Recovering home base. I say again, recovering home base."

"Roger, Snapper one two. Control understands you are recovering to home base. Thank you. Control out."

Shell begins a climb to three thousand feet and turns to a heading for Tempsford.

Only the best pilots fly the Lysander special-operations missions, for they must fly for hours at night by dead reckoning, with only their wits to direct them. That more aircraft don't get lost is a testament to the skill of those chosen as pilots for each mission.

Shell is feeling good about himself when, after hours of flying, he comes out almost directly in a straight line with his home base. Yet, he feels a little dwarfed by what John has done, for John's earlier statement that began "Sometimes they..." means to Shell that this isn't the first time John has done this sort of thing. Shell is impressed and intends to squeeze John for details when he buys him breakfast at the Officers' Mess. He wonders if Uncle Arch knows what John is doing.

Upon landing, he taxis the aircraft to an out-of-the way parking spot behind a hangar, shuts down the engine, and raises the cockpit cowling. He helps John down from the rear cockpit and is surprised to receive a rather significant hug from his cousin.

"Now about this 'What do you Brits call them?' comment you made," Shell begins. "I'm not a Brit, not even a bloody Canadian," he says, pointing to the Royal Canadian Flash on his left shoulder, which, of course, John cannot see clearly in the half light of the early morning.

A car pulls up, the rear door opens, and an American Army major general emerges. Shell sees him and snaps to attention.

John glances over his shoulder. Although he sees the general, he ignores him and begins to rag Shell about his uniform. "We've been in the war for almost three years, and you're still in the RCAF! What's with that?"

"Mr. Cameron," the general interrupts, "I'm from General Eisenhower's staff. Did you get the…" He turns and looks at Shell, dropping his head slightly and lowering his voice, as if doing so will negate Shell's presence. "The, uh, details?"

"Yes, General, I have them."

Mr. Cameron? Shell wonders to himself. A major general is calling John "Mister"? Maybe John really is some kind of a muckety-muck.

The general has taken John by the arm and is almost pushing him into the back seat of the staff car, the door of which is being held open by the general's driver.

"Got to go, Shell. But still, why the RCAF?"

Just before the car door closes, Shell manages to get out, "I'll tell you the next time I see you!" He salutes as the car drives away with its bumper-mounted two-star flag trying to fly in the heavy wetness of the early-morning mist.

But Shell would not be wearing an RCAF uniform the next time he saw John.

CHAPTER 24

IRONY

Dear Judge Cameron,

Thank you for your letter of April 4th. As for my health, I am as well as anyone could be in this business where reams of good, solid dialogue are written only to be shredded by directors and producers just as secret war messages might be after having delivered their undesired information. The writers are tasked to evoke this emotion or that, but the words we provide are seldom sufficient for the director or the producer, who look for one quotable line after another. They aren't really concerned about the overall movie but about whether the moviegoer will walk away from the theater quoting lines they've heard. That's what sells movies: people using movie lines as catchall phrases. And they expect us to come up with them.

If we know the actors who are going to portray the characters, it becomes somewhat easier to write appropriate dialog, because we have seen them act on-screen and understand what words and emotions they might handle better than others. But if a movie isn't yet cast, then we're dealing with unknown quantities and qualities, knowing full well that we will have to rewrite for specific actors' capabilities once the movie is cast. With someone like Joan Crawford, for example, you write no words but have her answer with a facial expression. But Gary Cooper doesn't do emotions, so you have to come up with something else. You see, it isn't just writing; it's visualizing on paper—and I have to say that movie directors and producers make book editors look like tame house dogs in comparison.

Irony of ironies, I'm currently working on a screenplay for Hemingway's *To Have and Have Not*. It's going to take some good acting to carry the abbreviated sentences the producer wants in the movie. I would rather be writing my own work, but we have to pay the bills, and most of my novels and books are out of print, although I have begun talks with Malcolm Cowley about what he calls *The Portable Faulkner*. I would like to think it's an original concept, but he has already done one for Hemingway. Still, any press that might convince publishers to dust off some of my older works is welcome.

I was intrigued to hear that your nephew Shelby had "followed my lead," as you put it, and joined the Royal Canadian Air Force. I hope he is well and by now back in the States with our Army Air Forces.

I was more surprised to learn that your Joshua is training Negro pilots in Montgomery. I'm sure there's at least a short story there—and probably a damn good novel. I'm thinking of Negro pilots and Negro officers. But I have some questions: Do they have their own officers' clubs? Do enlisted white men salute them? Are they integrated into the white culture, or do they have a separate-but-equal side of the fort? Is the training program solely for Negroes, or do whites go through the same scheme?

Perhaps this is the *deus ex machina* that young Joshua was expecting out of the war, the one he wished for the morning we had our after-hunt breakfast. Only time will tell, I suppose, for this war cannot last much longer. Hollywood is a good indicator of things future, and already we are inviting scripts for postwar movies. I think musicals might make a comeback, and you're going to see many more Technicolor films—not just the big-budget ones, mind you, but more middle-of-the-road films. Still, I think that what some directors can do with black and white will make the switch over slower, for Technicolor robs nuance, and nuance is everything to a story. For example, I mentioned writing for Joan Crawford's facial expressions; well, the success of those facial expressions is due in no small part to the lighting in a black-and-white movie. In Technicolor, all that disappears. Yes, Technicolor will make writing for the movies even more difficult. But I reckon there'll be lots of difficult things to come with the end of the war. Hopeful things, but difficult nonetheless.

My best to Miss Julia.

Sincerely,

William Faulkner

CHAPTER 25

BIGGLES VERSUS THE DOODLEBUG

August 1944, England

"BIGGLES! LEAVE THE MOLE ALONE! Quit digging!"

The Airedale–Fox Terrier mix looks up only long enough to let his owner know that he has heard him. Then, as if to say, "I hear you, but I'm a terrier, and this is a mole, one of my sworn enemies," he returns to furiously digging at the mound of earth, which is where the mole was last sighted. At least that's what his well-practiced nose tells him.

"Oh well," Shelby says to the young WAAF—Women's Auxiliary Air Force—officer seated next to him on the bench. "He's happy, but I'll have to bathe him later, and he isn't going to like that."

"Biggles, come here." The WAAF officer's voice has a decidedly Irish lilt. The dog looks at her, turning his head to the side as she pats the bench next to her. Then he trots over,

---

pausing only once to look back at the molehill, as if to say, "I have better things to do." Jumping up on the bench, he places his head in the lap of the WAAF officer, who gently scratches him between his ears. He closes his eyes and is asleep within moments.

"I swear, I thought I was the only one you had that kind of control over. Are you sure you're not a witch?" Shelby looks genuinely perplexed but happy. He leans over to kiss her but quickly draws back as two enlisted WAAF cadets pass by and salute. He stands and returns their salute but then leans over and kisses the auburn-haired young lady demurely on the cheek. More intimate goings-on can wait until they are alone this evening.

He sits down again, luxuriating in the sunshine that has become so elusive in what has been a cloudy, cool summer. He pushes the gray-blue cap backward on his head to allow the sun to reach his forehead.

"It's almost as if there isn't a war raging just across the channel," he muses to the girl. Well, she actually isn't a girl, for she is more than a year older than he is. Still, at twenty-three, she seems just a girl. She isn't Parisian-model beautiful, but she is attractive. Her auburn hair has decidedly red highlights in the sun, her green eyes are clear and mischievous, and she has inviting lips, perfect teeth, and a smile that coaxes one in return from whomever she encounters. But it is her freckles that give her that certain something. You don't notice them until you are up close, for they are small, but they are plentiful and give her face the look of a young lady who knows her mind, knows what she wants, and is content with herself. That she has reached the WAAF-equivalent of a squadron leader speaks to her abilities and drive. That she has fallen deeply in love with the young American seated next to her is very apparent to anyone who watches her watch him.

It is also apparent to any who even cursorily look that the young Royal Canadian Air Force squadron leader is completely and utterly in love with Miss Stella Donovan; and there are those who, watching him adore her, might also consider the possibility that she *is* a witch, so completely in her thrall is he.

He leans in to her. "Stella, I think we need to talk about some things."

Biggles hears it first. His head rises from Stella's lap, then he rises fully and, looking upward, barks. Shelby stands and, using his hand to shade his eyes from the seldom-seen sun, sights it coming in over the Channel at about three thousand feet. It sounds like a loud motor with a cylinder that keeps cutting in and out: *Bzz, pop! Bzz, pop! Bzz, pop!* It is a bomb with stubby wings and what looks like a stovepipe on top. From the stovepipe, a spurt of flame accompanies each pop.

"It's a buzz bomb." This from Stella. "Biggles, hush!" she commands. But Biggles continues to challenge this annoying threat to his perfect day.

"It's no danger to us; judging from the direction it's going, I think it's only going to make a hole in some farmer's field," Shelby says, trying to be reassuring. The recent increase in the number of German V-1 flying bombs has begun to make Londoners nervous.

"I see Special Squadron hasn't destroyed all their launching facilities." Stella's comment is wryly delivered, but her smile softens the sting.

Shelby takes her seriously. "No, I'm afraid they're rather easy to conceal—just a building or two and a ramp. We've bombed and strafed several of those closest to the coast, but it's those farther back that are getting these rockets off. Bloody things are fast too. Almost four hundred miles an hour. We can't catch them from behind."

But Stella doesn't want to hear about the specifications of the buzz bomb, or "doodlebug," as some people have begun calling them. Somehow calling them by a stupid name seems to lessen the power of the terror the weapon causes. Still, she doesn't want to talk about the war.

"You were saying we needed to discuss some things. Like what?" She turns her back on the doodlebug, even though Biggles continues to challenge its right to be in the skies over Kent.

The perfect day ruined, Shelby isn't about to ask her to marry him accompanied by the *Bzz, pop! Bzz, pop! Bzz, pop!* of a German V-1.

He balks and says, "Things. Just things."

Stella takes his hands in hers and, looking upward into his steel-gray eyes, asks, "Do you mean like making an honest woman of me? Things like that?" She looks for a moment as if she is about to pout, but Squadron Officer Donovan does not pout. Stepping back half a step but not letting go of his hands, she declares, "Shelby, it's time we were married."

"Oh, damn. Damn! Damn!" Shelby does not seem pleased, but then he takes her right hand in both of his and, kneeling on the public byway, says, "This is not at all how I had planned it, but, Squadron Officer Stella Donovan, will you marry me?" He delves deep into the inside pocket of his tunic and produces a small blue box. He forgets to open it before handing it to her.

She takes the box, opens it, removes the ring, and hands it to him. "You're supposed to put it on my finger," she reminds him. He first tries to put it on her right hand. "No, darling, this finger," says Stella, holding out her left hand.

And all the while, Biggles continues to run in circles, barking at the now departing doodlebug and its *Bzz, pop! Bzz, pop! Bzz, pop!*

CHAPTER 26
Mosquito versus Doodlebug

"So, TELL ME MORE ABOUT this wedding you and Stella have planned." The navigator looks up at Shelby from his seat to the right of and below the Mosquito pilot.

"Nothing big. Just some of the gang from our squadrons. Of course, I have to get some leave first so I can visit her folks in Ireland and ask their permission."

"So, no big wedding in Ireland or New Orleans?"

"Nope. Just a small one at St. Thomas Church in Canterbury—although I know my mother would be happy if we would wait until after this show is over and have one in St. Louis Cathedral in Jackson Square in New Orleans. And I'm sure Stella's parents would prefer their local parish in Enniskillen."

"St. Thomas, you say? That's right, you're not Church of England, are you? St. Thomas is Roman Catholic, named for the old archbishop himself, isn't it? And you say Miss Stella isn't one of the Protestants from the north of Ireland but a Catholic herself. Well, that does make a nice fit for you, doesn't it?"

"Uh-huh." Shelby is only half paying attention to his navigator's chatter. He is scanning the horizon, hoping to pick up intermittent spurts of flame from the exhaust of a V-1. He knows Roland is scanning as well, but Shell finds the chatter a bit of a distraction.

"We were Catholics once, you know. Family's from Normandy. St. John is English, even though we still use *Sinjan*, which is the French pronunciation." Roland doesn't normally chatter like this. He only chatters when he is nervous. Shell doesn't see this mission as any different than the previous twenty or so they've flown over the past two months, so he doesn't understand Roland's nervousness. Lord knows, though, that any twenty-year-old should be nervous with a twenty-three-year-old at the controls in an aircraft hunting a nineteen-hundred-pound flying bomb.

"Thought you were all Catholic until Henry the Eighth?" Shelby inquires about the obvious.

"Umm, yes. Well, there is that, I suppose." Roland leans to the right with his hands cupped against the canopy, squinting into the blackness toward the Channel.

Shelby reaches for the rheostat to dim the cockpit lights even further than their already pale-red glow. After all the low-level night missions he and Roland have flown into France and Germany and all his Lysander missions for the Special Operations Element, he is used to flying with the cockpit completely blacked out. Even now that he is flying over the friendly territory of the Channel and the coast of England, he still prefers to fly in as dark a cockpit as possible. It isn't that he is concerned someone on the ground will see him but rather that the darker it is in the cockpit, the easier it is to discern the pinpricks of light that indicate terror weapons inbound. The farther out they can engage the doodlebugs, the less the possibility that someone on the ground will be injured by the falling debris of the 1,900-pound bomb that constitutes the majority of the body of the V-1.

"Come right twenty degrees." Roland's matter-of-fact tone is no different than the one in which he made his last comment about Catholicism.

Shelby banks the aircraft, rolling out twenty degrees to the right of his previous heading.

"Should be at our twelve o'clock, below us." Roland is peering ahead into the darkness.

Then Shelby sees the glow as the V-1's pulse jet pushes a dragon's tongue of flame from its engine.

"Tallyho," Shelby acknowledges to Roland that he has sighted the enemy machine, and then keys his radio transmitter.

"Control, F-for-Foxtrot. Tallyho Bandit, twelve o'clock low, current position, approaching coastline, engaging. I say again, tallyho on Bandit."

"Roger, F-for-Foxtrot. Understand engaging. Good hunting." The control radio operator responds as a WAAF plotter places a small block of wood with a V-1 placard on the plot table in ground control and pushes it out onto the map in the sector that F-for-Foxtrot is patrolling. If F-for-Foxtrot has spotted a V-1 in its sector, it is likely that other aircraft will begin to spot doodlebugs in theirs, for the bugs come in swarms.

While transmitting, Shelby has maneuvered his Mosquito farther to his right and then back to the left so that the incoming V-1 will be obliquely off his nose when approaching from his right. He does this to maximize the target profile. Were he to engage head-on, he would be shooting at a much smaller silhouette thereby lessening his chances of hitting it with enough firepower to destroy the missile. This way, when he fires his cannon, he will have the entire length of the V-1 to shoot at as it passes through his sight line. Through all this mental figuring, he has had the aircraft descending from ten thousand feet to the three thousand feet of the incoming threat.

"Cannon are bore sighted for three hundred yards." Roland reminds Shelby that the four twenty-millimeter cannon in the aircraft's nose will converge their streams of rounds three hundred yards in front of the nose. At a combined closure speed of over five hundred knots, Shelby has only a microsecond to do damage to the flying bomb.

"I say, Shell. Won't this be number five for us?" Roland's matter-of-fact confidence in him makes Shelby feel more confident himself, but he doesn't answer. He concentrates, trying hard to mentally project the flight path of the V-1 and throttling his engines back slightly so that he doesn't overrun his planned intercept. He gauges maximum range and presses the firing button on his yoke, unleashing his four Hispania-Suiza twenty-millimeter cannon and four Browning .303-caliber machine guns. Together, they fire 4,600 rounds a minute, but

Shelby does not have a minute, or half a minute, or even ten seconds. He is approaching the V-1 on a collision course and can see that several of his tracer rounds have found the weapon. When his Mossy is three hundred yards from the terror vehicle, the twenty-millimeter shells find their target and the flying bomb explodes, sending glowing shrapnel through the night sky. Shell pulls back hard and pushes the yoke to the right, attempting to lift the Mossy away from the red, yellow, and white explosion, but the aircraft shudders as pieces of the V-1 slice through the laminated plywood of the Mossy's airframe.

Shell hears Roland yelling, but he is now fighting an aircraft that wants to fall off on its right wing. His starboard motor has exploded and taken part of his right wing with it. Smoke billows into the cockpit as Shell struggles to keep the control yoke in his hands. The uncontrolled gyrations of the aircraft keep trying to wrench it from him. He tries to keep the Mossy upright, but she keeps wanting to skew over to the right in a steep bank. His initial thought is to feather the propeller on his starboard engine, but even though he can't see through the smoke, he realizes the prop is gone, taken off in the explosion. After what seems like minutes but is in reality no more than twenty seconds, Shell realizes the aircraft is no longer going to fly to his command.

"Bail out! Bail out!"

It's up to Roland to open the escape hatch, which is down by his seat. Shell fights to control the aircraft and feels a rush of air fill the cockpit as Roland gets the hatch open and goes through it into the incredibly bright light of the burning engine. Shell struggles to attach the bungee cord to hold the yoke in place so he can leave his seat, but the aircraft fights him. Finally, he secures the cord, but he has no reason to believe it will hold the yoke against the aerodynamic forces long enough for him to slide from the seat, squat on the wing spar, and launch himself into the night. But it does. Just as he pushes himself out of the small hatch, the aircraft lurches sharply to the right, and he sees the tail of the aircraft coming toward him; he ducks his head, but the elevator strikes him solidly.

CHAPTER 27

HOMECOMING

April 1945, New Orleans

THE PLATFORM IS CROWDED AS the Panama Limited slowly pushes into the terminal at Union Station. There are uniforms everywhere; soldiers in khakis, sailors in white bell-bottoms, and Navy and Marine Corps officers in sand-colored summer uniforms. It looks like the entire population of New Orleans is in uniform and standing on Platform One in Union Station. Still, blended into the crowd, there are more than a few suits and dresses as civilians wait to greet their loved ones and business colleagues arriving from Chicago, St. Louis, Memphis, and other points north.

The day cars, which were added to the all-sleeper setup at the start of the war, are pushed closest to the terminal. After those come the twin dining cars and the Pullman sleepers; then, farthest from the terminal, come the baggage cars. The train slows even more, crawling the last few feet, and then, with a clattering of car stopping car, it halts. White-coated porters in their black, high-crowned hats swing down from the doors of each car placing boarding stools so that passengers can step from the train onto the platform. Greeters swell toward the exit doors, each searching for a face or faces in the crowd.

Soldiers and sailors spill from the day cars, adding to the swirling undulation of the uniforms on the platform. Then another set of uniforms flows into this kinetic art piece as black-coated baggage handlers with their high-crowned red caps push hand trucks and trolleys through the crowd. The red caps call out, "Careful there, coming through! Watch your feet! Excuse me, sir. Pardon me, ma'am."

Standing by the dining cars are Judge and Mrs. Cameron, Mr. and Mrs. Devereux, and Little Arch, who uses his height to look up and down the platform.

Now, almost as if a director has struck the podium with his baton, silence cascades down the platform from back to front. Movement ceases. First heads, then bodies, turn toward the back of the train. Four red caps wheel a baggage cart on which lay two flag-draped coffins. People shuffle out of their way as the red caps approach. The Judge removes his Stetson; there are tears in his eyes. He offers his pocket kerchief to his wife, whose tears run down her cheeks. The soldiers and sailors come to attention and salute. Civilians place their hands on their hearts, and all of them turn to follow the cart's progress toward the terminal.

"Well, at least they've come home. So many fellows don't." The voice is from behind them. "Too many are just buried where they fall, and many, especially aircrew, aren't buried at all. But at least these families will have some closure." The voice is deeply resonant.

The five turn away from the departing caskets to see a tall man in a Royal Canadian Air Force blue serge uniform and a tallish, attractive young lady in a blue-gray Women's Auxiliary Air Force tunic and skirt. The man leans heavily on a cane with one hand and holds the leash of a black-and-tan dog with the other. The dog is standing as calmly as a two-foot-tall being can stand in the sea of legs that has now begun to churn again. A still-angry, red scar runs across the bridge of the man's nose and extends downward under his left eye, but there is no mistaking his face. It is thinner now, but it is the once-cherubic face of Shelby Devereux. The auburn-haired WAAF officer carries leather gloves, which are so completely out of place in New Orleans in April.

Now the tears on his aunt's face, his mother's face, and his father's face are those of delight and relief. Shelby has come home.

From the silence of the bubble that has surrounded the scene, Little Arch says, "You missed Mardi Gras again this year, but we froze you some king cake, and I kept some coins for you."

CHAPTER 28

BACK ON THE FARM

"HE SIMPLY WON'T GO BACK to university." Stella rocks gently on Uncle Arch's porch while Biggles lays with his head off the edge. His tongue hangs from the side of his mouth as he luxuriates after having chased a bevy of squirrels around the side yard. "Says he doesn't need it to eventually take over the family business, but I know what he really means is he doesn't want to be in a class of eighteen-year-olds." She pauses to sip at the teacup from the side table. "You can't really blame him, of course. How does a twenty-three-year-old man go backward and become an eighteen-year-old again? I mean, we hope to start a family in the not-so-distant future." She sips again, looking into the distance at the woods that surround the fields next to the house.

Uncle Arch, unsure of just how she finds hot tea refreshing on an already sweltering May afternoon, considers the condensation on his glass as he notes that the ice in his tea has watered down the strong Darjeeling brew he prepared. He might not care for hot tea in the summer, but he is somewhat of a tea aficionado and prefers a strong mountain tea to the weaker

Lipton and Jewel packets of blended lowland tea leaves. Like his tobacco, he orders his tea and coffee from an importer in New Orleans.

"Well, he's pretty much right on both counts. He doesn't need a college degree to run the Devereux businesses, although some accounting and related business courses might be a good thing. He also doesn't need a college degree to study law. Mississippi and Louisiana still allow people to read law under the tutelage of a good lawyer. We can put him in a firm in New Orleans as a clerk, and he can read for the profession. As long as he can pass the bar, he can practice law. If, of course, that is something he would like. I presume he is thinking of my life as he considers whether university is important, but he might have forgotten that I had my degree before I went off to war. Still, he's right that colleges these days are geared to educate youth—not to train men." Uncle Arch does not sip at the tea in his glass, rather he takes a long swig.

"I hope that once we have finally dealt with the Japanese, that situation might change, given the influx to the colleges of all the returning GIs we'll have. Still, I suspect the universities will resist and want the GIs to conform to the ages-old traditions and customs of academia. We'll see."

A humming from the north increases in volume until the Stinson roars low over the green fields and pulls up to clear the house as Shelby and Little Arch announce their return from Memphis.

The Judge continues. "I had a note from William Faulkner— the writer." He describes the man for his new Irish niece. "He says the Army Air Corps has already begun demobbing the Hollywood men it had drafted into its motion-picture brigades. Says they're all showing up to the studios expecting their old jobs back but with an increase in pay for the experience they've gained working for the army. He says it's somewhat of a humorous situation since these men never actually left Hollywood but were just drawing pay as corporals and such while they did their jobs as cameramen, scenery builders, lighting and sound operators, and such for the army film units. It's like one day they come to work in a khaki uniform, and the next day they show up in khaki pants and a short-sleeved cotton shirt expecting to restart their civilian lives. The studios are having a hard time of it because during the war they hired 4-F draft-deferred status men to replace these fellows on the movie sets, and now the original men are wanting their jobs back.

"Shell's not the only one with readjustment issues. It was the same with the last war, and I suppose it will be the same with any future war. How do you go from the regimentation of military life to a 'you're on your own' civilian life? And, more importantly, how does shooting straight, knowing how to throw a grenade a goodly distance, or spotting an infiltrator coming across the wire translate into making a living in a world not at war?

"And that's just those who come back whole. We have so many wounded with permanent disabilities, and then there are those whose souls and psyches bear the invisible scars inflicted by combat. It will be a great challenge for us as a nation. How well will we treat these men and women? How well, indeed?"

He stands and moves to a switch beside the double front door. Flicking it, he looks upward at the porch ceiling over the chairs in which he and Stella are sitting. "No reason to have all this good government electricity and not use it." He watches the three porch ceiling fans as they slowly start their circuitous courses around their respective electric motors, gaining speed until they are swishing a goodly breeze downward onto a grateful Biggles.

"Not too much wind, is it, Daughter?" He addresses Stella in a familiar, familial manner.

"No sir, just about right, I would reckon." Stella bats her eyes slightly as she slips into the accent. Just a few days and she has become a family member, able to take on the Judge in his own arena.

"Just 'I reckon,' not 'I would reckon.'" He corrects her.

"I *reck-on.*" She splits *reckon* into almost two separate words, the Irish lilt in her voice giving the sometimes caw-like southern expression a musical quality.

"Much better," he laughs, as he finds his chair again.

As he watches the beads of condensation roll down the long glass of iced tea, he remembers the difficulties of soldiers returning from the First World War and considers how much worse the coming decade will be, because this time so many more men and women experienced the horrors of combat. His grandfather bore the scars of the Indian Wars and his father the scars of the Civil War. And he himself limps on cool, humid days when the piece of metal in his knee gets cold. "Just how many generations of wounded will this country produce?" he asks himself. It is, decidedly, a problem to ponder, but at the moment he is only concerned with two returning veterans—Shelby and Stella Devereux.

He sips at his tea, then lifts his glass and, to no one in particular, toasts the Rural Electrification Authority for their real gift to the South: "Thank you, REA. Thank you, Mr. Roosevelt. Thank you all for the gift of ice." And then, as an afterthought, he adds, "And, oh yes, those ceiling fans are nice too. Thank you for them as well." Putting the glass back on the arm of his planter's chair, he continues his conversation with Stella.

"We had a letter from John last week. He's back in Washington for a bit. I still don't know what he's really doing, but he seems to be coming through this mess without being too much in harm's way. At least that's what he tells me. And his mother is grateful for not really knowing, or at least for being able to believe that he isn't at risk."

"Yes, sir, I'm glad of that." Stella knows what John is doing and just how much in harm's way he has been, for Shelby told her about his brief encounter with his cousin. But, of course, she cannot tell the Judge. That is John's story, and it is up to him to tell it.

"You need a new plane. Something faster than that outdated cabin cruiser; something with two engines for safety. I mean, I kept rocking backward and forward the whole trip, trying to get that airplane to go faster. Why, they have trainers now that are faster than either the Stinson or the Waco."

"Sure. And you probably want it to have .50-caliber machine guns in the nose."

"Fifties? Sure, why not? Although I'd prefer a twenty-millimeter cannon with explosive rounds. Much quicker than having to pump a lot of lead into your opponent just to hit something vital."

Shell is using his hands—cane held up in his right—to demonstrate one aircraft diving on another. That he continues to walk as he does so indicates to the Judge that the injuries to his thigh and hamstring are healing well.

Little Arch, walking alongside, watches Shelby's hands then suddenly reaches out and grabs them between his own much larger appendages.

"Stop that! You're going to make me dizzy. You act like my students trying to explain a barrel roll. They always forget the twenty-degree offset at the beginning and end up describing a slow aileron roll instead of a barrel roll. I swear, all the hand flying makes a man plumb dizzy."

Both men laugh as they make their way up the stairs of the porch.

"And has my fiery-tempered Irish wife been telling you how to run the county?" Shelby directs the question to Uncle Arch as he leans down and gently kisses Stella's cheek, his hand on her shoulder. She, in turn, takes his hand and kisses it.

Little Arch drags two more rockers into the conversation area and plops himself down in one. "Lordy, Lordy, Lordy! I thought I was back training those 'I don't know nothing 'bout flying' trainees! Young Shelby here almost killed us three times—and me almost a married man. I tell you, Judge, I don't think we should let him up in the aircraft alone. No, sir, I don't believe Mr. Shelby here is ready to solo yet." His laugh is big and fills the porch. Biggles looks up, startled from his afternoon nap, but seeing no action lays his head back over the edge of the porch and resumes his dreamland hunt, wherein he actually catches the squirrel he is chasing.

"You been making tactical approaches and such again, Shell?" Uncle Arch looks serious. "You know that airplane isn't certified for aerobatics. Pull too many g's, and the wings will come off."

"Tactical approaches? Me?" Shelby places his hand on his chest. "Not me, no sir!" He sounds incredulous.

"Well, remember one of the first things I taught you." The Judge is serious and is using his "from the bench" voice. "A pilot never exceeds his capabilities or those of his aircraft. You may be an excellent pilot, but that aircraft is almost ten years old and isn't certified to be flung about the sky. You want a newer, more capable aircraft? Then either get your father to invest in one or find out what you want to do, do it, and buy one. But don't you kill yourself or anyone else in my airplane." He speaks sternly, but then, in a voice less stentorian, follows on, "You remember my friend Bill Faulkner?" He stops long enough for his listeners to remember and for him to swig at his tea.

"Well, his life was completely changed when he sold his Waco cabin cruiser to his brother Dean and then Dean went off and killed himself and some others because he exceeded his abilities. The Waco was too much airplane for him, and Faulkner has never forgiven himself. I'm sure his heavy drinking is due in part to his trying to escape the guilt he feels. Now consider how I would feel if I let you fly my aircraft and you went and killed yourself doing something the airplane isn't designed to do. Think how the young missus there would feel." He nods his Stetson-covered head at Stella, who looks at Shelby with an imploring look that clearly says, "Please listen to him."

"Yes sir, I understand." Shelby's acceptance sounds sincere, but the Judge wonders whether the next time Shelby flies he will try to push the aircraft beyond its limits once again.

"Well, just as long as you do." The Judge leans forward and pushes his Stetson back, revealing his still-sturdy shock of hair that—although now completely white—is the envy of most men his age. "And you may be right; we may need a new airplane. I suppose in a few months there'll be a lot of military-surplus aircraft available. Maybe we should think about what type we need and be on the lookout for something. And no, we don't need any Mosquitoes, Bristol Beaufighters, or P-38s."

The Judge then turns the conversation to business. "Joshua, how did we do up around Memphis and in Arkansas?"

"Well, pretty much just what you said, Judge. The military is cutting way back on its contracts for delivery of lumber, but there's an underlying feeling that as soon as they start lifting price controls, there's going to be a big housing boom. A lot of people are holding on to their trees anticipating the government action, but we're still in with most of the folks with whom we've been doing business. I assured them we would be competitive, and most of them gave us a first refusal right to bid."

"Good." The Judge takes his pocket kerchief and, holding his Stetson by its already grimy crown, uses the kerchief to swab the leather band inside the hat. Placing the hat back on his head, he notes, "First, we have to see about getting a couple of good peeling knives, because there's going to be a tremendous call for plywood, and I want to be able to produce the necessary wood elements for the plant. Shell, your daddy is going to set up another plywood plant, and we'll make exterior-grade plywood for all these builders just like we've been making marine-grade plywood for the Higgins boats. Then we'll need to see about lining up the right labor for the various jobs. Everybody who worked for us during the war stays on. Nobody gets replaced, but all the new hires will be veterans. And as for hiring the veterans, let's make sure we take combat vets over the behind-the-lines, 'I served too' people that will be applying. We'll need some training courses and safety courses for the new hires. Shelby, you want a job? Since this is a joint Cameron-Devereux project, we can put you in charge of hiring. It isn't as exciting as flying a Mosquito in combat, but it's a damn sight safer, and I'll bet we pay better than the Royal Canadian Air Force." The Judge laughs and—reaching over—slaps Shelby on his good knee. "Welcome back to the real world, son."

That night, in their room at the end of the house, Stella lies with her head on Shelby's chest, her left leg up over his torso and her hand tracing lightly the curve of his cheek to his chin. The slowly turning ceiling fan churns the warm, moist air made even warmer by their lovemaking.

"Please listen to Uncle Arch. Don't push the airplanes to do things they can't. I love you. We came through the worst, and we've earned the best—so let's enjoy it. This is a good world, Shelby. It's your world, and now it's my world, and I like it. I like the people, I like the place, I like this time, and I like us. Talk to your uncle. He'll help you let go of the war, and I'll help you grab on to the future."

She rolls over on him once again, her lips fastening to his, his head in her hands, and her heart in his.

CHAPTER 29

TALLYHO! TALLYHO!

October 1960, Near Richmond, Virginia

THE SMALL MAN SITS ASTRIDE a large bay horse. He sits the saddle well enough, although there is a slight slouch noticeable to the more experienced of the riders who gather for the early morning hunt of the Farmington Virginia Hunt Club. The man wears a hard bowler hat, a herringbone hacking jacket, and a white-silk scarf gathered inside his jacket and secured with a gold tie pin. He is up and ready as the hostlers bring around a tray of silver cups and offer them to the riders. He leans down, lifts a cup, and, as he brings it to his lips, notices a new rider decline the hostler. The new rider reaches into his outside jacket pocket, retrieves a flask and, removing the top, swigs a draught from the stylish pewter container.

The new rider—a man not yet middle-aged, sitting tall in the saddle, wearing an expensive Donegal tweed riding jacket and a soft dark brown Trilby—catches his eye. "Prefer my own. Could never stomach that Pimm's concoction." And holding up his flask offers to pour a portion into the silver cup from which Faulkner has already drained the Pimm's.

The liquid is a slight golden color, and as Faulkner noses it, he discovers the soft smell of freshly cut peaches. After the heavy taste of the Pimm's and the coating it left on his tongue, this new elixir seems light yet strong, formal but cheerful. The taste is a familiar one, but Faulkner cannot remember from where the familiarity comes. Before he can ask, the Master of the Hounds is sounding the call, and the pack of foxhounds is moving off. Faulkner upends his cup, still trying to identify the original in his memory. He hands the now empty cup to a hostler and guides his horse into the group of riders. He has lost sight of the new rider, who must have fallen in behind him. Well, there will be time after the hunt to explore the origin of the golden elixir and the well-seated stranger.

It happens quickly; the hounds move out, casting about for scents, and then a leader yelps as he takes up a trail and the yelping becomes the bay of the hunters. "On! On!" the riders urge as they spur their mounts to follow the hounds. "On! On!" And as the pack of hounds breaks a hedge and begins to climb the side of a hillock, the red fox is suddenly visible in front of them, its tail even redder in the slanting, early-morning rays of the late-October sun.

"Tallyho! Tallyho!" The shouts ring out as the riders spy the fox. And now the fox clears a small stone wall that has been in place since well before the Civil War; and now the dogs clear the same wall, followed by the lead riders, their red coats showing the way. Faulkner's horse makes the jump, barely lifting himself. It is no challenge. Faulkner is forward in the saddle, his form not perfect, but he and the horse remain one even if there are crevices of light between his bottom and the saddle. He does not lead the riders, but he is not so far behind the front-runners that he cannot keep their red coats in sight. The fox takes them over a three-rail split-rail fence. Again, Faulkner charges it as if it protects a cannon in the valley before Sebastopol. Again, no tragedy befalls him as the large horse clears the top rail. "On! On!" the riders cry.

Some do not attempt the fence, rather riding along it to achieve a gate. They fall behind, but Faulkner rides on, an aging cavalier chasing the demon Roundheads from the field.

A hedge, another fence, a small brook— "On! On!" A larger stream, another hedge—onward the fox rushes until it can go no more. The dogs reach him first as he turns, exhausted, to defend himself. The handlers are there quickly; they wade through the dogs and, grabbing up the carcass, lop the fox's tail. Faulkner reaches the dogs just behind the leaders. He pulls his charger up at the edge of the yelping pack of hounds. There is lather on the horse's flank, and Faulkner sits back in the saddle, breathing hard but beaming. He is still up, and he is in at the kill.

CHAPTER 30

AFTER THE HUNT

THE HOSTLERS HOLD THE REINS and help the riders down from their saddles. Some use the mounting block to dismount, as Faulkner does. As his horse is led away, he notices the new rider sling his right leg over the horse's neck and slide off his saddle, catching himself nicely as he lands, bending his knees just so. Still, as the tall man walks away, there is the indication of just the slightest limp on the right leg. Faulkner follows him into the clubhouse.

Stowing his hat and riding crop in a cubbyhole, the tall man pulls at the bottom of his jacket to seat it properly on his shoulder and then turns for the dining room, which is serving a hunt breakfast buffet.

In the dining room, he goes first to the coffee urns, draws a cup, and then selects a small table very near a window with a view of the Blue Ridge. As he sits:

"Excuse me," Faulkner makes his approach.

The man looks up from his coffee and stands. "Why, Mr. Faulkner! Or should I say Professor Faulkner?" The tall man offers his hand.

"Mister is fine, but I'm afraid you have the advantage of me." Faulkner shifts his crop from right to left and takes the proffered hand.

"As would practically everyone these days. That is, everyone who reads or sees *Life and Liberty* magazine covers on the newsstands." The tall man pauses. "I'm Shelby Devereux."

"A pleasure, Mr. Devereux. May I ask from whence comes the golden elixir you offered me before the hunt? Somehow I find it familiar but I'm having some difficulty remembering where I've tasted it before."

"Well, you might have had it in one or more of the better restaurants or hotel bars in New Orleans, but I think you may have shared a glass with my Uncle Arch when you breakfasted with him in 1938. He often spoke of your praise for Miss Julia's biscuits."

"Oh, of course. Of course! And how is the Judge? We haven't exchanged letters in many years."

Faulkner remembers the breakfast well, now that his memory has been jogged, and he wonders why he and the Judge have not corresponded. When had they lost contact? Maybe around the time of the Nobel Prize and all the hoopla that surrounded it. Yes, he reassures himself. It was all that folderol of the Nobel. Yet, in castigating himself for losing contact, he still feels the pleasure of the Nobel Prize wash over him, as it has many times in the past decade.

"And Miss Julia, of course. I do remember those biscuits."

"Well, Miss Julia is fine, Mr. Faulkner, but I'm afraid we lost the Judge last fall. In fact, a year ago next week."

"My goodness!" Faulkner is taken aback. "Was it his heart? We seem to have any number of people having heart attacks these days."

"No, not his heart. Like his life, his death is an intriguing story. If you'd like to join me for breakfast, I'll share the details. I was just about to go through the buffet."

"Well, if something like that doesn't pique one's interest..." Faulkner lays his riding gloves on the table and steps off toward the buffet, Shelby Devereux in train.

Returning to the table by the window, they carry plates laden with scrambled eggs, hominy grits, and large, fluffy biscuits. Faulkner accompanies his eggs with bacon while Shelby has a large slice of fried scrapple fresh from a Virginia farm on the Eastern Shore of the Chesapeake. The scrapple isn't often found at Southern breakfast tables, but it is about as close to boudin sausage as one gets in the north of the South, as people from Mississippi and Louisiana refer to Virginia, Tennessee, and Kentucky.

Once seated, Shelby begins. "It was late October last year. The Judge had been foxhunting the night before, and it had taken more time than usual to collect his dogs. They had gathered all the dogs but one, and the Judge, Little Arch, and John—John's my cousin, Uncle Arch's son; he was a spy with the French underground in the war—well, anyway, they tramped through a goodly bit of the countryside, over deadfall trees and through a number of blackberry-cane hedges, before they finally found him. His collar had caught on the branch of a dead pine tree that had fallen in amongst a big bramble, and he couldn't get it loose. Uncle Arch fell a couple of times as he made his way through the bramble of canes, upturned tree roots, and such, but finally the dog was loose and back in the truck with his brothers, sisters, and cousins." Shelby stops to take a bite of the scrapple and egg, nodding his head slightly to indicate that he thinks them tasty.

"I remember the morning we looked for the dogs. It seemed to all go very smoothly those many years ago." Faulkner fills the silence of Shelby's chewing.

"So, then the three of them—that's Uncle Arch, Little Arch, and John—had breakfast at the house, and then they went to Uncle Arch's office to talk some timber business. John says Uncle Arch seemed fine, although he put on his old purple college cardigan sweater with the big shawl collar that he kept in the closet instead of wearing his normal canvas house jacket. It was cool out, but not abnormally so—but apparently Uncle Arch kept folding the shawl collar up as he leaned over his desk and he had the fire in the fireplace built up so that John and Little Arch had shed their jackets.

"The three of them spent about an hour in Uncle Arch's office, and then Little Arch headed out to check some timber work that was being done up toward Laurel. John started back to the house he and his wife Lara built on the back side of the farm. Before he left, Uncle Arch asked him if he wanted any quail, because he had seen the evidence that a covey or two had taken up residence down by the cornfields where the corn was drying on the stalks before harvest. Uncle Arch said he was going to take the dogs down and shoot some birds, and if John wanted any, he should mention it now otherwise the Judge would just shoot enough for himself and Miss Julia and maybe one or two extra unless, of course, there was a real bevy, in which case he just might shoot a bunch and hang them in the smokehouse." Again, Shelby stops long enough to fork some eggs and scrapple into his mouth and chew them; then he takes some biscuit and follows that with a swig from his coffee cup.

Faulkner asks, "So he still had bird dogs? I remember he had—what was it? Oh, classical names for the two I met. Antony and Cleopatra or something like that."

Shelby, looking over the top edge of his coffee cup, laughs. "I think you're remembering Tristan and Iseult. No, this pair is Tallulah and Barrymore. They've since taken up residence with John. Tristan and Iseult are buried down in the meadow with all the other bird dogs and foxhounds who have lived on the farm.

"Anyway, as John was leaving he told his father he thought he looked a little pale, to which Uncle Arch replied, 'That's from you keeping me in the office too long with all your new ideas of how we should be running the businesses, you and Shelby...' Oh yes, I come in for my share of blame here." Shelby smiles at Faulkner with a "Well, you know the Judge" look.

"Then the Judge said to John, 'You and Shelby, with your ideas of expanding production, growing soybeans, and extracting vegetable oils, plant fibers, and methane gas instead of gasoline and such. You'd think we were poor or something the way you two carry on. I'm fine, and after I shoot a bag full of birds I'll be better.'

"After John left, Aunt Julia says Uncle Arch came into the parlor where she was working on smocking a christening gown for whichever grandchild, niece, or nephew would come next. As he leaned over to kiss her, she thought his skin felt cool but she put it off to perhaps his having been outside. She didn't realize he was coming from his office and a built-up fire. And she noticed that he was limping more than usual so she asked him about it and he answered that he was stiff from having to fetch Conniption from a blackberry bramble. He assured her it was nothing to worry about, winking at her just before he closed the door.

"So, he apparently took his heavy field coat from the mudroom, as well as his over/under twenty gauge, a pocketful of bird-shot shells, and an over-the-shoulder game bag, and headed down through the meadow and off to the west toward the cornfields. It wasn't long after that that Aunt Julia heard several shots from the west, and she began to think about quail recipes. John heard some shots as well and wondered just how many birds his father was shooting.

"Well, now, Uncle Arch and Aunt Julia had this system where they used referee whistles to communicate when he was out on the farm. One tweet to get your attention and you answer a tweet; then I can tell you what I want by the number of tweets. Several short tweets in a row is emergency; two long slow tweets is mealtime; one long and one short means there's somebody at the house who needs to see you—and so on."

Shelby stops for another sip of coffee while Faulkner nods his head, his lips pursed like he is thinking, 'that's a pretty ingenious system.'

"So, after a while Aunt Julia goes to the kitchen to fix some lunch and when it's just about ready she goes out to the west-facing porch and tweets for Uncle Arch but there's no answer. She waits and tweets again, and then a few minutes more and again. When there's no answer she goes in the house and telephones John.

"Well, I could draw out the search story about how Little Arch showed up pretty much with John and how they headed off to the cornfields looking through the rows only to find Uncle Arch on the far side at the edge of the pecan orchard sitting with his back to the trunk of a very old pecan tree. Tallulah and Barrymore lay very near him; Tallulah with her head across his legs. The Judge looked as if he might be napping, but he wasn't.

"When John tried to find a pulse, there wasn't one. So, there he sat—Stetson on his head, his arms at his sides. By his left hand was his small writer's notepad. When John picked it up he read: 'Feeling light-headed / leg swollen bad / stiff / knee won't bend / should whistle but left the damn thing in my housecoat / not heart attack just feel funny, like flu coming on but very cold / maybe rest will put me right / drank some brandy / need to get birds cleaned / hung up.'

"At his right hand lay his flask and the shotgun, broken open with the barrel pointed away from him. John said it would have made a perfect painting: *The Hunter in Repose.*

"So, the doctor did a partial autopsy and discovered a small piece of metal in Uncle Arch's leg had worked its way into one of the branch arteries just behind the knee and Uncle Arch had slowly bled out. As the doctor said, as far as he was from town, then trying to diagnose the issue and prep for surgery and get Uncle Arch's A-negative blood donated, they might or might not have saved him. As it was, the doctor said, there wasn't much pain, just a gradual sleepiness and being cold."

Faulkner sits silently, his eggs mostly pushed about on his plate, for he has eaten little during Shelby's telling of the Judge's death.

"The metal?" he asks, suspecting he knows the answer.

"The metal was a piece of shrapnel from a wound in the First World War. Floated around in his knee for more than forty years. It's no bigger than half a picayune, but it was big enough to punch a hole in the artery. Miss Julia has it mounted under a magnifying paperweight so you can actually see it up close. It's on the Judge's desk, which, save for the paperweight, is just the way he left it that morning."

"Yes, I remember he told me about that piece of metal when we visited in his office. Said he didn't want to risk paralysis of the leg to have the doctor attempt to remove it. Yes, I remember." And Faulkner thought back to that one meeting with the Judge. He remembered how guilty he felt in the presence of a real wounded pilot; or had it been fear of detection of his deception that he had felt? It was an odd emotion, guilt or fear? Perhaps it was both.

"I am sorry for his death. I remember him as a unique man. A man who was always willing to give quarter but would never think of asking it for himself. Perhaps a man too much in advance of his time. His life would make a great novel. Perhaps it is something I should write." Faulkner muses a moment, perhaps thinking about the opening paragraph he could write. Shelby watches him contemplate and then breaks the silence.

"He was decidedly a unique man. It's hard to categorize him. He was more than even a Renaissance man. I'm not sure we've yet defined a type for Uncle Arch. I like to think I could be like him, but he was genuinely one of a kind. How many people do you know who have four funerals?"

Faulkner sits up. "Four funerals?"

"Oh yes, four funerals. One at the Episcopal church, one at the African Methodist Episcopal church, one at the Mount Olive Baptist Church, and one at the Mount Zion Baptist Church. And, if you count the memorial mass my mother laid on at the cathedral in Jackson Square, five."

"Well attended?" Faulkner cannot help but ask.

"People standing in the aisles. Well, at least at the first four of the services. Not as large a turnout in New Orleans, but that funeral was much bigger than I thought it would be. Two hundred people or so. The Negro churches in Mississippi each insisted on having their own memorial service for him. Lord, they said such things about him I was sure his resurrected self was going to come through the doors of the church and down the main aisle. The Episcopalians didn't do nearly so much. They just did the service for the dead and had a memorial communion. The bishop came in from Jackson and wanted to do the eulogy but John wouldn't let him. Instead, he and Little Arch mounted to the pulpit to eulogize their father and surrogate father. It was strange to see Little Arch in the pulpit of an all-white Episcopal church. It made many of those in the congregation a little less than comfortable. I saw many of them cringe when Little Arch mounted the steps, and there was more than a smattering of whispered questions and observations in the congregation—but when Joshua began to speak in that resonate baritone voice of his, they all quieted down and paid attention to what he had to say about how their lives had been better, more prosperous, and safer because of the Judge. Before he stopped, he reminded them that there was little doubt that God would have the Judge sitting on heaven's judicial bench and that each of them should keep in mind just how well the Judge knew each of them. How's that for exercising power from beyond the grave?

"The Episcopalians were a little miffed we didn't bury him in their cemetery." Shelby waited a moment for Faulkner to take that in and then said, "Buried him with the dogs. He did so love those dogs."

Shelby puts his knife and fork on his plate and pushes back just slightly from the table. He takes the pewter coffeepot a waiter had left on the table and fills his cup, offering first to warm Faulkner's. He then replaces the pot on its trivet and, reaching into his jacket pocket, takes out his flask. "Would you care for a little more of Uncle Arch's brandy?"

In the time between the appearance of the flask and the word "brandy," Faulkner takes his unused water goblet and places it in front of Shelby who uncaps the flask and pours an ample serving of the amber liquid into the smallish, stemmed glass. Shelby then tips the top of the flask toward his coffee cup. "It would seem a sacrilege, but it does the coffee a world of good." He smiles, returns the flask to his pocket, and then offers up his cup in a toast. "To Archibald Cameron, a unique man."

"A unique man," Faulkner echoes, raising his glass to touch Shelby's cup.

He swirls the brandy, then sniffs it. The smell delivers him back to the Judge's office of 1938. He remembers—a unique man certainly, but perhaps a dangerous man as well.

"So, the Negro churches held their own memorial services, you say?" Faulkner asks.

"Absolutely. It was as if no other service was being held. I was impressed. I had always known my uncle was well respected among the Negroes, but the outpouring of grief was overwhelming. Grown men were crying." Shelby looks into the distance above Faulkner's head, seeing in his mind the sights of the church funerals and hearing once again the gospel hymns as people celebrated and mourned the Judge at the same time.

"Yes, I would have thought as much," Faulkner sips the golden liquid, enjoying the warm burn on his palate and the effusion of warmth as the effects of the brandy spread through his body. "Yes, he was a man of the colored people and, I suspect, of the small-farm whites and sharecroppers as well. He could have been another Huey Long if he had wanted to be. They shared an antipathy for the klan that was reciprocated tenfold." Faulkner holds the water goblet as he might a crystal brandy snifter, but then remembering the Judge's admonition about crystal and brandy, considers that perhaps this plain glass was all this elixir needed.

Shelby watches the writer appreciate the brandy. "Oh yes, the Judge could have been much more important than he was, but that was one of the things I admired most about him. He was content with who he was, what he was, and where he was. As for the klan, he had pretty much gotten them under control in the '40s and early '50s. He had riddled the organization with rats and moles and agents provocateurs. He knew, sometimes before orders had been given to the local wrecking crews, what the klan planned, and he was usually able to cause some kind of disruption. Of course, he did a lot to show that klan activities during the war were un-American and could be interpreted as impeding the war effort; and after the war the klan was slow to pick up steam again. So, it wasn't a problem until a few years back when integration became an issue. Then it kind of exploded, but by that time the Judge had retired from the bench. Some of us do what we can to counter the klan's influence and, as in most cases where political issues touch emotions, sometimes we succeed and sometimes we don't. I still hope that eventually we will grow out of such childishness, but given the march of human nature I fear we may not. There will always be klan-like groups. Fact is, I'm surprised you haven't had more trouble from the klan, Mr. Faulkner." Shelby sips at the cup.

"I've been following your career with interest, and of late I've noticed how you've been a little more outspoken than many Southerners on the plight of the Negro. And that because of your outspokenness you have become somewhat of a—if you'll forgive a feeble attempt at humor—black sheep in parts of the South. In other words, celebrated for your success in the hallways but castigated for your views on the Negro in the salons off those hallways."

Shelby watches Faulkner's eyes closely. He sees indecision. Faulkner isn't sure how he should respond. It is true that in his time at the University of Virginia he has answered questions and made some statements about the inequality and poor treatment of Negroes, but he has steadfastly refused to take a stand on what should be done to remedy the situation. Shelby has read the transcripts of Faulkner's small question-and-answer series at Virginia, and although Faulkner is much more candid than most Southerners about the Negro problem, he hasn't, by any means, called for major societal changes. He seems only willing to say that changes are needed and that the Negroes are deserving of better lives, jobs, and educations.

Faulkner has chosen his answer. "Yes, but I must say that things here in Virginia are not as dire as they seem in Mississippi. There are some Negroes in the law school and a few in the undergraduate college, although certainly not in the proportions one would expect to find if integration were truly the law of the land. And I now spend much of my time here." He does not repeat his previous comments that the Negro will have to be allowed to assimilate into the white culture, or say that, in his opinion, the Negro has a lot of work to do to achieve that assimilation.

Shelby understands they will not discuss the issue of the Negro further at this moment. Faulkner's 'and I now spend much of my time here' is definitively stated. He might as well have slammed his glass down upon the table to emphasize the finality. But one does not slam a thin-stemmed glass down upon a table.

Faulkner, the cool of the morning charge across the fields having awakened his senses and the touch of the brandy having awakened his mind, at last remembers. "Oh! *You're* the nephew the Judge said had taken a page from my book. The one who went to Canada and joined the RAF."

"The one and the same, but it was the RCAF. The Canadians are a little sensitive about that, as I'm sure you're aware. It was the RCAF. They like to have the Brits remember they're Canadians, especially the French-speaking crews of the RCAF. Still, I did most of my flying with elements of the RAF during the war.

"I left New Orleans by train and went to Chicago and then to Toronto. Since I was eighteen I didn't need my parents' permission to sign up, and when I showed the Canadians my flying logbook and spoke French and German for them... well, *voilà*, as our French cousins say. I bypassed basic training and went through the advanced flying portion in an accelerated course—only having to learn the proper air force terms and military etiquette. I thought I'd be posted overseas immediately, but because of my fluency in French they held me back as an instructor for French-speaking students. So, while I didn't go through basic myself, I had to sit in the back seat with a lot of ham-fisted students crying '*Incroyable! Zut! Zut! Zut!*' or just '*Merde!*' as they tried to kill me four times a day while bouncing our training aircraft off the runways. I managed not to die for six months and then the RCAF put out a call for experienced French-speaking pilots for some mission or other they were planning with the RAF. I was selected along with four others, and the five of us checked out in the twin-engine Bristol Beaufighter, but just before we were to leave Canada for England they cancelled the mission. I never found out what it was. Still, I was shipped overseas with a Beaufighter squadron to North Africa where I became part of the Allied Air Forces contingent attacking German shipping in the Mediterranean as they tried to resupply Rommel. The Beaufighter was a really good antiship aircraft, and we sunk most everything we saw. After a while the Germans stopped trying to resupply during the daylight hours and switched to night arrivals for their ships. So, the next thing I know, the medicos are giving the lot of us more eye tests, and then a group of us are designated 'night flyers' and we're sent off to find and attack the German shipping at night.

"I did that until we beat Rommel and invaded Sicily. Then they posted me to England where I retrained on the new Mosquito fighter-bomber and found myself flying special night missions attacking targets in France and Germany. Sometimes we flew pathfinder missions for the RAF heavy bombers where we would precede the bombers into Germany and mark the designated targets with flares and small incendiary bombs so the Lancaster bombardiers could see them. That meant we had to be spot-on when we dropped our ordinance, otherwise the Lancaster missions would be in vain. It was pretty nerve-racking work, but it was better than having the bombers drop their bombs blind. Mostly, though, we attacked special targets like Gestapo buildings, German airfields, and fuel dumps—sweeping in low-level under the German radar and using our speed to evade the German night fighters on return. It was a lot safer than attacking those places during the day because at night the antiaircraft gunners can't see you—especially if there's no moon or there's fairly low cloud cover.

"For a very brief period I flew relief for the special-mission Lysander pilots who were flying agents into and out of Europe. Actually ran across my cousin John on one of those flights. I swoop into France to pick up this fellow and it turns out to be John, who was with the Office of Strategic Services working with the French underground. That's how I came to find out he was a spy.

"Then I went back to special missions in the Mossy, and we were shooting down the German buzz bombs until I got too close to one and…well, now here I am."

"Here you are?" Faulkner is more than curious. "'Here' is in Virginia. Your narrative stopped in England. How does one get from England to a Virginia foxhunting club? And you stopped your story in 1945, but here and now is fifteen years later." Faulkner expects more.

"Well, 'here' is easy. I was left with a pretty stiff leg after the war and I couldn't run. Since squash and tennis were out of the question I took up riding, first with longer stirrups and then, as I became more flexible, with shorter stirrups, until I could actually post in the saddle without falling out. Then I started jumping, and one thing led to another, and here I am chasing foxes in Virginia. As for the Farmington Hunt, I do business or sit on boards with several of the permanent members and have a standing invitation to hunt as a guest during the season. I also have friends in the Keswick Club and some other riding establishments throughout the southern and middle-Atlantic states.

"I doubt Uncle Arch ever mentioned my father to you, but we're in sugar, rice, timber, and such. The family has been in New Orleans since before it was part of the United States. My mother is Uncle Arch's baby sister.

"We do a lot of business with the government in Washington so I come down to Charlottesville whenever I'm up here in Virginia or the District. Anything to get away from those politicians with their hands out and their wagging tongues. What's that old joke? How do you know when a politician is lying…?" Shelby sips from his coffee cup, pausing to enjoy the mingled taste of black coffee and brandy. "When their lips are moving." He smiles and takes another sip. "Still, it is our government, and we have to pick sides and try to do what's best for the country."

As Faulkner is about to reply, a throaty roar from the parking lot interrupts him.

"I think that's my wife," says Shelby. "She's picking me up so we can get back to Georgetown tonight for a reception for Senator Kennedy."

Faulkner looks out the window and spies a tallish woman with auburn hair under a teal-colored headscarf lifting herself from a decidedly un-American convertible. The car is larger than Chevrolet's Corvette but not so large as a passenger sedan and certainly not as large as the Ford station wagon he himself drives. It is painted a shiny gun-metal blue. The woman, the car, and the not-so-distant Blue Ridge Mountains are framed within the gold swag of the window dressing. It looks like a travel poster.

CHAPTER 31

DRIVING WITH STELLA

"SORRY TO TEAR YOU AWAY from Mr. Faulkner, but you know this evening is important if we're going to help Jack get elected." Stella makes a run up behind the car in front and swings out to pass the sedan, downshifting the Maserati out of overdrive so that the car produces an almost musical bass chord when she steps down on the gas pedal. She expertly eases back into the right-hand lane and pushes the speed up well beyond the sixty-mile-per-hour speed limit. Stella likes to drive fast. Traffic is light this morning on US Highway 29, and she is taking advantage of the open road. With the top up, the Maserati is much quieter than other convertibles.

Keeping her eyes straight ahead, she observes, "I have to say that when you introduced me, all I could think of was how much like a small porcelain figurine the great writer looked. That silver hair, the mustache, the riding jacket and breeches, the polished boots, and that pipe. He reminds me of a small statuette my aunt had on her fireplace mantel. I think it had 'The Squire' inscribed on the base."

Shelby is amused. Stella is a shrewd observer and has nailed Faulkner's newest role in one try. "Yes," he answers, "Faulkner has found a role that suits him and for which I think he has yearned his entire life. Uncle Arch told me once that he thought Faulkner wanted to be his own great-grandfather. A fearless, larger-than-life type who built railroads, took risks, and ended his life in a duel in the streets of Ripley, Mississippi—if I'm not mistaken, and I'm not."

Shelby smiles at his wife as she gauges another victim for the Maserati's dual-carburetor engine and rack-and-pinion steering. She hangs back, matching the speed of her victim; then, when she sees an opening, she downshifts and throttles up—picking up speed and closing the distance with the car in front of her. At passing speed she eases the car into the left lane, passes, and then quickly and smoothly is back into the driving lane and once again into overdrive. She maneuvers the car as if she were racing at Monte Carlo.

Shelby, lips pursed, nods to compliment her driving and then responds to her observations. "Faulkner's given name, William, is after his great-grandfather, who was, among other things, a semifamous novelist—although he had only one book that was a bestseller. I think the *White Rose of Memphis* sold more than 150,000 copies, which, for the nineteenth century, was a goodly number of books. Hell! It's still a goodly number of books! But there's no question in my mind that Faulkner believes he is now his great-grandfather...good ol' Colonel Sartoris himself. But given our brief conversation this morning I doubt he's about to be shot down in the streets of Oxford or Charlottesville because of a personal animosity based on his politics or business practices. More likely, he's going to fall off a horse and break his neck. I swear I've never seen a luckier rider. Faulkner should have fallen off three times—or more—but somehow he managed to stay on. He charged every jump like it was a life-and-death situation. The reason he didn't fall was the horse. He's a big, talented horse, but the Lord will have to do more to keep 'Colonel' Faulkner in the saddle if he gets a skittish, less accomplished jumper under him."

"He's really that bad?" Stella sounds surprised.

"Not bad…" Shelby thinks about walking back his observation but says instead, "Not bad; it's just that he thinks he's better than he is, and that's about the worst thing that can happen to someone using a skill where lives are at risk. I saw it first when I was instructing new-pilot wannabes. They'd get a good report from an instructor on one ride and the next thing you know they'd be trying to do things well beyond their capabilities. And that gets you into spots you can't get out of. That's why the most deaths occur among low-time pilots. It's the same in combat. The longer you live, the more you learn, and the more you learn, the longer you live. But the whole concept is predicated on knowing your limits and accepting them."

As Stella slows the car approaching the town of Warrenton, Shelby is boarding the train of thought following the analogy he had just used and muses, "I wonder if Faulkner flew airplanes the same way he rides horses? I'll bet he did, and I'll also bet that he did something that gave him a good scare and that's the reason he stopped flying. He's scared so he stops flying and he sells the airplane to his younger brother Dean who proceeds to kill himself and others trying to do something beyond his skill level. Now how would that make Faulkner feel?"

Not knowing the question was rhetorical, Stella glances over. "Pretty damn rotten, I would imagine. I mean wouldn't you feel awfully guilty that whatever it was that scared you might have killed your brother? You'd be forever asking yourself, 'What if I had just sold the damn airplane to somebody else?'"

Shelby nods in agreement, then concludes, "Well, let's hope a horse scares our writer before he's thrown over a jump."

Stella pulls the Maserati into a head-on parking spot outside a diner on Main Street. Inside, the two slide onto a red, plastic-covered booth seat and order tomato soup and grilled cheese sandwiches. Stella asks for a Coke, and Shelby asks if they have Royal Crown Colas. They do.

"So, Shell, will you go back and ride with Mr. Faulkner again? Maybe hint to him that a lesson or two might help him stay in the saddle? We don't have to be back in New Orleans right away, do we?"

"If you mean could I do something that would convince Faulkner that he isn't as skilled as a dragoon at jumping his horse over hedgerows, the answer is no. He's much too deep into the persona to listen to anyone. It's in fate's hands now. Either he realizes it himself or he doesn't. Foxhunting doesn't have evaluation boards like military aviation does."

Stella is giving him the 'I've-seen-you-do-harder-things' look she gives him when he is obstinate about doing something she thinks needs doing.

"Look, Stella, even civil aviation doesn't have the ability to intervene beforehand to strip someone of their pilot's license. Either they realize they're a danger to themselves or they don't, and if they don't then fate either lets them stumble through without death or serious injury or, conversely…" He sips from the straw he has dropped in the neck of the RC bottle.

"But you could try, couldn't you? I mean, even if you don't go back to Charlottesville this week you could write him a letter."

"Yes, dear, I suppose I can write him a letter thanking him for the conversation, but you've got to be careful stepping in between a man and his fate. For all we know Faulkner may be pushing his luck in hope of a gallant death."

"Pish tosh!" is all Stella can muster.

"No, dear, you have to understand." Shelby has taken on his serious 'now-listen-here' tone. "If Faulkner believes his role calls for him to die a gallant death…" but here Shelby stops and begins not talking directly to Stella but musing aloud, "Still, if being scared is what stopped him from flying…"

"So, you'll write him a letter?" Stella is insistent.

"Yes, a letter." Shelby relents. "Besides we didn't have time this morning for me to get into the questions I wanted to ask about his novel *A Fable* anyway.

"I didn't like it." Stella swallows too quickly and coughs, sipping her Coke to aid the grilled cheese on its way. "It was too dated for me, and I don't really see soldiers stopping in the middle of a war like that. I mean, think of what would have happened if our soldiers had suggested to Hermann Goering's division that they should all throw down their arms." Stella is finishing her soup and looking for the check. She's anxious to get back to Georgetown.

Shelby knows that Stella, in her indomitable fashion, has once again cut to the heart of the matter. "Yes, that's it. Faulkner chooses the only war where his plot is plausible, although I could see it working perhaps during the Civil War as well...but certainly not during the latest fracases we've fought. Of course, there is that story of the first Christmas Eve in the trenches in World War I, where the Germans and British stopped fighting long enough to celebrate the Holy Day. Still, imagine our marines trying to work something out with the Japanese soldiers on Iwo Jima or with the Red Chinese soldiers in Korea. 'Hey! Let's put our weapons down and meet for tea.'"

The check is five dollars and forty cents. Stella leaves seven dollars on the table. She's a big tipper. She waves to the waitress and slides out of the booth. "Yes, it would have been absolutely absurd in any of the latest wars, but I could see it in the First World War where it was predominately king-doms that were fighting one another, and there was always some internal latent animosity between the working classes and the aristocracy. The Bolsheviks got the Russian army to stop fighting, but it wasn't peace they were interested in, just power."

Shelby holds the door for her and then darts past her to get the door of the Maserati. He has done this since before they were married, and Stella appreciates it.

Stella announces their departure from Warrenton with another pipe vibrato from the dual exhausts of the Maserati. She resumes the conversation. "So why didn't he attempt to set his novel in a more current, more understandable time for the average reader?"

Shelby is not stumped for he has given this considerable thought. It was, in fact, one of the avenues of conversation he had hoped to pursue with the writer after the chance meeting on horseback. "Well, I think some of it has to do with just being 'Faulkner.' I mean, he *is* a Nobel Prize–winning author, so everything he writes is going to be read and critiqued at least by the literati, and their reviews will be in the *New York Times* and other literary and political instruments of communication. So, Faulkner writes an antiwar novel. It's the antiwar part that is important. There is a Christ-like figure who is executed for his preaching which sets the common man against the elite. My understanding is that Faulkner worked for a decade on the book—meaning he must have started it before the end of World War II. I can think of any number of reasons why he wouldn't have chosen that war, but primarily because for the United States it was a great crusade against evil. He would have been pilloried had he had US forces in World War II laying down their arms. But, as you point out, World War I was about kings and queens, and tsars and emperors. Three of them were even cousins. The only two republics involved were France and us; and we came three years late to the commotion. Yes, I have lots of questions for Mr. Faulkner. Perhaps I will go back to Charlottesville next week. Somehow his antiwar posturing strikes me as very similar to his position on the Negroes. He has a general position suggesting that something needs to be done, but he isn't brave enough to come out and say what. He makes his antiwar statement about a past war in a world very different from our current one."

"That's interesting, dear. I think you should pursue it. Uncle Arch would have wanted to know, I'm sure." Stella is concentrating on the heavier traffic as they near the outskirts of Alexandria. Shelby, though, does not watch the traffic; rather, his mind is on whether Uncle Arch might not have already known, for he feels his uncle had taken the measure of the writer early on.

CHAPTER 32

A RECEPTION IN GEORGETOWN

THE ROOM IS LARGE, WHICH is surprising, because the house appears almost modestly small from the street. The decorations and furniture are federalist, which means, of course, that the sofas are terribly uncomfortable to sit on. But one does not sit at these soirees. One stands—drink in one hand, cigarette in the other—and one chats and watches. Shelby does not like these receptions and goes only because Stella is very much involved with the Democrats and somehow knows Jacqueline Kennedy, who is the wife of this year's Democratic nominee, Senator Jack Kennedy. Of course, that the Kennedy family is Irish and Catholic has not escaped his attention, and—as Stella had predicted way back in May—Kennedy won the Democratic nomination. The only thing that troubles Shelby is Kennedy's running mate, Lyndon Johnson. Shelby is more than a little familiar with the senator from Texas and does not trust him any further than he can spit into a forty-mile-an-hour wind. Thankfully, the running mate will not be here tonight.

Shelby fiddles with his pipe to avoid being drawn into any number of what he considers inane conversations by hangers-on in their college ties and signet rings. The cigarette smoke suffuses the room, swirling behind people as they move about. It reminds Shelby of condensation trails from his engines while at altitude. Leaning over just a little so he can whisper in Stella's ear, he says, "This is what they mean by politics being done in smoke-filled backrooms. I wonder if someone is being offered an ambassadorship for a little extra contribution to enable more television time for the candidate."

Stella is having none of Shelby's cynicism. "Of course someone is being offered an ambassadorship. Politics is business; and you, as a successful businessman, should appreciate the art of the deal." She elbows him slightly in his ribs. "Besides, this isn't a backroom; it's at the very front of the house." She smiles "that smile" at him, and he is, once again, content to just be at her side.

But the mood is broken quickly when Mrs. Kennedy motions Stella to join her and her husband. Ignoring someone trying to get the senator's attention, Mrs. Kennedy takes her husband by the elbow and, turning him slightly, says, "Jack, I'd like you to meet Mr. and Mrs. Shelby Devereux of Louisiana. Stella has been a big help in organizing get-out-the-vote events for you throughout Louisiana and in Virginia as well."

Kennedy offers his hand first to Stella, who takes it and smiles. "I'm sure you're going to win." Her Irish accent, although tempered by fifteen years in the South, is still pronounced, and Kennedy picks up on it immediately.

"Do I detect a lilt from the auld sod?" His Irish accent is terrible, the clipped Massachusetts harshness cutting off the softer Irish tones.

"Indeed you do, but I'm through and through an American now—or as much an American as any other immigrant. Shelby has seen to that."

"Well, we're all immigrants in some form or another." Kennedy is politic. "And you are Shelby." He offers his hand and Shelby takes it, shakes it once, and releases it.

"Nice to meet you. We've great hope for your presidency." He does not feel any electricity from the candidate; Jack Kennedy's eyes are lively, but they roam around the room searching out potential allies who might need more persuasion to dig deeper into their bank vaults for the cause. Shelby is disappointed. He had expected at least to like the fellow; but while the smile is engaging enough it is a stage smile—a politician's smile. The tan is even but underneath there is a sallowness. Still, Shelby does like what the man claims he stands for, and his victory might offer some relief from the same old politics of the South, which have become mired in wannabe demagogues' interpretations of "the cause" as equivalent to states' rights. Yes, Reconstruction had been a crime and the Depression only made matters worse, but times change and one either changes with them or becomes the detritus of history. Shelby is ready for change—well, at least political change—and this fellow promises it.

Before any other chitchat can be exchanged, one of the erstwhile young men present sidles up to the candidate and whispers something sotto voce. Shell catches, "…local television station."

"Excuse me." Kennedy apologizes to the group of three and moves off following the aide toward the back of the house. Just for kicks, Shelby follows in the candidate's train, drawing up at the doorway to a room in which is gathered a group of ten or so men all watching a figure on a twenty-one-inch Zenith console television. One man turns to tell Kennedy, "Harry Byrd is making an address on states' rights and this local Virginia channel in Arlington is carrying it. Can't tell really well, but it looks like the *New York Times* and *The Washington Post* are both there."

Shelby recognizes the speaker as Robert Kennedy, the candidate's younger brother. He has the same harsh, clipped Boston accent as his brother. Because the voices are both in the alto range, with their Boston intonations they sound almost whiny. Shelby finds it off-putting, but guesses they probably find his New Orleans accent equally unappealing.

"What are we going to do about this guy? He's going to steal a bunch of votes. It seems he's got a bunch of these appearances scheduled between now and the election." Robert is more than a little exercised that Senator Byrd is running as an Independent against the very things John F. Kennedy says the Democratic Party represents. "Damn it, the Civil War was over a hundred years ago. Where does this guy get off preaching segregation?" Robert is mad.

"Ninety-five years ago, Bobby." Jack corrects his little brother. "Ninety-five years ago."

"What? What's ninety-five years ago?"

"The Civil War ended ninety-five years ago—not a hundred. Besides, Byrd's not on the ballot in Virginia." Jack is pulling Bobby's chain in an attempt to calm him down, but it doesn't work.

"Damn it! I don't care if it was fifty years ago or five years ago! Where does Byrd get off with this segregation and white-power shit? What are we going to do about him?"

"Well, you could always put a skunk in his car."

"What?" Jack Kennedy, along with those clustered around the TV, turns to face the tall stranger, who leans against the doorjamb as if it needs a flying buttress. "What did you say?"

"Skunks. They're very practical and also very symbolic. My uncle used them very effectively against just such a phenomenon as Senator Byrd."

Jack Kennedy is intrigued. "Really? And just how did he do that?" Kennedy is glad to have the attention drawn away from Bobby.

Shelby, seeing no reason to enter the room, simply straightens himself in the doorway—which his shoulders pretty much fill.

"Well, my uncle was a county judge in Mississippi, and he had all sorts of problems with the klan. Yes, I said the klan—and make no mistake, gentlemen, you're dealing with the klan here. The only people who are going to vote for Byrd, or Faubus, are supporters of the klan; and, contrary to popular belief, the klan does not rule the South nor even does it have a major say in our politics. But I digress. So, my uncle, over the years, had recruited a number of klan members onto his payroll. Mostly he recruited them by not sending them to jail for various offenses and then controlled them with the threat of possibly doing so at some future date should they fail to adequately perform the roles of spy or agent provocateur against the interests of the klan." Shelby pronounces *agent provocateur* with his French accent.

"So, on this one occasion a source tells him the klan is planning a big conclave in a heavily forested area almost in the middle of the county. Now, Uncle Arch—that's his name, Arch—now he tells this source that he has to volunteer to be the guard the klan leaves once they put up the cross that is to be burned during the meeting. Then Uncle Arch and my cousin Little Arch go out and trap a bunch of skunks; must have been ten or eleven. Now, catching skunks is pretty easy; really, you just load up the trap with some salt pork that you've left in the sun a day or two, put the trap out about sundown, and by midnight you'll have a skunk—or maybe a pretty mad raccoon—but mostly you'll catch a skunk. The tricky part of skunk hunting is to get them out of the cage without getting yourself sprayed, but with some experience you learn how to do it.

"So, Uncle Arch and Little Arch take the skunks to the clearing the afternoon before the klan meeting. With the help of my uncle's klan agent they pull this hollow tree trunk out of the truck and put it on the edge of the clearing and then they put the skunks into the tree trunk and close up the end with a big knot of wood held in place by a sturdy stick wedged between it and the ground. Then they pull a slab of putrefied salt pork from the tree trunk all the way across the clearing and hide it under some grass and sphagnum moss.

"Now the agent has his instructions—he is to stand near the tree trunk and when the kleagle has the members all whipped into a shouting frenzy the agent is to kick the stick away, releasing the skunks.

"Well, the rest of this I have from piecing together multiple accounts of what went on, for you can appreciate that no one is going to tell the story as if it was a firsthand account since they don't want you to know they're in the klan; but it seems these skunks—now mind you, they haven't eaten for a couple of days, and they've been cooped up in that log together, and skunks aren't very sociable animals—well, anyway, they've been smelling this salt-pork smell for some hours now, so when the knot falls away from the opening they come out like swamp water from a spigot, all black and oozy. They try to follow the scent of the pork, but there are all these people in the way and then somebody yells 'Skunk!' and there's running and jumping and the robes swirling around and such. Well, these skunks are powerful mad and powerful hungry—and they perceive all this activity as a threat…so, well, you know what skunks do to defend themselves. They start spraying." Shelby stops to allow the imagery to form in the minds of his listeners.

"Now I don't know how many of you have ever seen a skunk spray, but it comes out like a fan—kind of like those water sprinklers you see on lawns. I mean they actually can direct it, and generally they'll aim for the eyes of a predator—but these skunks just sprayed it all around. Well, you've got all these klownsmen flapping about in their white robes running hither and yon trying to get out of the path of these skunks—who by now are running in all directions trying to get away from all these large flapping things. Skunks have really bad eyesight, so all they can see are these flapping images, which for them may signify owls or such. Anyway, there's spray going off everywhere in the clearing and people running off into the darkness of the woods and others making for their cars. People screaming as they get hit by the spray, people kicking at the skunks, which, between you and me, isn't a real good idea because it will only make the situation worse. Then someone takes out a shotgun and starts trying to shoot the skunks. Well, I mean, discharging a shotgun in the middle of a crowd is really going to make an already panicked throng panic even more...and it did.

"Well, there were a lot of prominent citizens missing from town the next week or so while the stink wore off. I suspect there was a big order for fresh white klan robes from whomever it is that supplies such things, and a lot of dogs avoided sniffing car tires for a while." Shelby pauses.

"So just put a skunk in his car. He won't make any appearances because he'll stink until well after the elections and people will avoid him...well, like the skunk he is."

Everyone is clapping, and Shelby bows from the waist. Another Southern raconteur has captured his crowd.

Kennedy waves him into the room and introduces him to the suits of his campaign.

"Have a good time?" Stella is almost elated as she wheels the Maserati away from the house.

"Depends upon your definition of a good time." Shelby is undoing his tie.

"I mean, did you enjoy meeting the next president of the United States? Did you feel the electricity of his ideas?"

Stella is a true believer. Shelby suspects that with Stella it is more about wanting to believe than actually believing, but then he asks himself, Isn't that what believing is about? Wanting to?

"To be honest, Stella, what I saw was a bunch of Ivy League guys and a bunch of old politicians plotting to win control of Congress and the White House. Don't get me wrong. I don't trust Nixon, and I wouldn't vote for him, but I bet that if we'd have gone to a party for him tonight we would have seen the same fervor and heard the same discussions, worries, and laments that we heard here. You said it yourself: politics is a business, and there are two groups competing to get the biggest contract you can ever get—running the US government. I've been to far too many of these events where someone wants to be a governor or a senator or even just a representative. They're all the same; it's just the office that differs.

"Idealism is like Uncle Arch described Faulkner's aviation writing. Makes a good story, but the real stuff is missing. What did Uncle Arch used to say? Where's the snot on the scarves and the vomit on the jacket fronts? What about the soiled pants and the sleepless nights where fear—not of death but of fire and disfigurement—keeps you rolling in your bunk? I admit that I enjoyed walking the streets of London in my blues with my wings and my medals—my DSO and my DFC—and I liked having people idealize me as a hero, but all the time I knew I was a fraud. All the time I was afraid of the next mission. That's the difference between idealism and realism, and I—my dear, darling Stella—am a realist."

"Oh, pish tosh! At heart you're every bit as much a romantic as I am. Otherwise I wouldn't love you so much."

Stella makes the corner and heads across the Key Bridge towards their home away from home in Arlington, Virginia.

CHAPTER 33

ON! ON!

"Ooh! This is too strong, Granddaddy. Who taught you how to make coffee?"

"Too strong? Coffee can never be too strong, young lady! I think all this living in the North has weakened your sense of taste."

"North? We've only lived here two years, and since when is Arlington, Virginia, 'the North'?"

"Since about 1960 when the Yankee lawyers started moving down here from New York pushing big-government programs. That's when."

"Granddaddy, that was eons ago. Let's see, if I do the math…Why, that's fifty-five years ago. How can you even remember 1960?"

"You'd be surprised how far back I remember, Shelby. You'd be surprised; yes ma'am, you would! Do you know that if I make another six years I'll be a hundred years old? No one in my family has ever made one hundred. Not one of the

Devereuxs, none of the Camerons, none of the Harmons, none of the Jourdains. No ma'am, not one!

"But as for remembering—well, I can remember back to about when I was five. That was 1926. And then too, I remember the stories my parents and grandparents told from their remembrances, and the stories they had from their parents and grandparents. Then my uncles, aunts, cousins, and so forth. It's a people thing—and very much a Southern thing. Remembering, that is. Remembering is an important thing in all cultures, but it's pretty much *the* thing in the Southern culture from which you and I spring. Remembering and doing—those are the two things I like most. Remembering and doing."

He holds the cup in two hands, looking at her through the steam. She is a tall, auburn-haired girl who, when seen through the rising steam, looks a great deal like Stella did when Shelby first met her. His great-granddaughter—who now sees only his eyes above the coffee cup and hears his strong, melodious voice—imagines him as a much younger man, perhaps as young as her father, his grandson.

"Well, speaking of Southern culture, what do you remember about Southern literature?" she asks, taking her tablet computer from its case and opening the cover. "I'm taking this course at Georgetown and we have to do a paper on William Faulkner. Personally, I would rather write about Caroline Gordon or Katherine Anne Porter. I'd like to concentrate on their conversions to Catholicism and explore whether those conversions had an impact on their writing—but the professor says that we have to do Faulkner. Why do you think that is?"

Before he can form an answer, the young Shelby continues, "He's too hard—Faulkner, not the professor. The professor is a real sweetie. He's from Pass Christian and his accent is to die for; all the girls think he's a real hunk. But Faulkner is too hard. I mean, his life isn't—although it's interesting and all that—but reading him is just too hard. It worries my head." The older Shelby smiles at the expression that has survived from Stella down through the grandchildren to this, his eldest great-grandchild and yet another namesake.

"Why didn't you ask your professor?" Shelby is practical in his quest for more information.

"Well, we did, and he said something about 'body of work' and 'impact on style and culture.'" She pauses, holding her touchscreen stylus up to her lips in a thoughtful pose. "Oh, and something about 'truly Southern.' What do you think that means—'truly Southern'?"

Old Shelby considers a moment. "Now, you see, there's an expression that requires prior knowledge. What have you learned in your course about the Southern Renaissance? For example, you mentioned two writers just now. Who were they?"

"Caroline Gordon and Katherine Anne Porter," young Shelby answers, her mouth full of toast and fig jam.

"There, you see. Gordon and Porter are considered part of the Southern Renaissance writers' group, but they weren't Southern in your professor's 'true South' sense of the words. At least, not considered such by those who are from the Deep South."

"I don't understand you. Not from the South?"

"Well, you see, those of us from the Deep South have different boundaries for what is the South and what isn't. For example, the Confederacy originally consisted of just six Lower South states and Texas."

"Wait—Texas wasn't a state? Yes, it was! Texas was a state! What kind of history did you study?" Excited, young Shelby is about to declare her great-grandfather non compos mentis.

"Calm down." Shelby holds up his hand, indicating she should wait for him to finish. "The South isn't as monolithic as outsiders believe. We've always had the Upper South, the Lower South, and Texas. The Upper South is Virginia, North Carolina, Tennessee, and Arkansas. Northerners will always put Kentucky in that group, and sometimes Missouri, because they were slaveholding states, but slaves don't have anything to do with the designation. Now, as for Texas being a state... Sure, Texas is a state, but when you refer to someone from Texas you don't call them a Southerner. You call them a Texan, and Texans always want you to remember that they joined the Union as a wholly formed and fully functioning republic and that they are, they believe, entitled to leave the Union at a time of their choosing. Now, they weren't the first republic to be annexed by the United States—that was the Republic of West Florida—which is part of Louisiana—but I digress." Shelby catches himself thinking too much of the history of the Gulf Coast and the filibustering that led to control of the region by the United States.

"Anyway, the South isn't a monolithic entity. It has distinctly different cultural influences in different parts. It is far less homogeneous than the northeast or mid-Atlantic regions of the country. The writers you mention are from Kentucky and Texas; they have different cultural and familial experiences than Faulkner, whose family is from Mississippi. For example, think of music—Dixieland, jazz, and the blues had their origins in New Orleans and along the river, up the Delta into Mississippi and Memphis. Gospel music came out of the Lower South in Georgia, Alabama, and Mississippi; and country music came out of the Appalachian Mountains of North Carolina, Virginia, and Tennessee. It originated in Scots-Irish familial traditions. Then, when you combined the tempo of jazz and the voices of gospel and country, you got rockabilly and then rock 'n' roll, and so forth. Lord only knows where the stuff they call hard rock came from.

"But my point is this: each section of the South has its own influences, and when you're looking for explanations of anything, you have to trace back through the various incorporations and amalgamations seeking the original source. The Kentucky writers you find in the group of Southern Renaissance authors were part of the Agrarian Movement. You can look it up on Google or Wikipedia. It was a group of writers who believed the agrarian lifestyle was superior to the industrial and that the South should look to its agrarian roots for the future. Look up *The Fugitives*, and you'll get a good start. But remember, Kentucky was spared most of the Reconstruction—not having to suffer under military occupation like the states that had seceded—so there's a big chunk of Southern history missing from their experience.

"You can listen to others describe their experiences during Reconstruction, but it's very much different when it's your own father or grandfather telling you your own family tales of personal loss and deprivation of rights as opposed to listening to someone else's relative telling his or her story. And make no mistake, Reconstruction was, in no small part, one of the reasons the South produced a generation of renowned writers—not unlike Ireland, where Irish writers prospered at a time when Ireland was occupied by the English. The impact of 'foreign' occupation, as it were, is one of those things lost to our current society, which always wants to view the past through what I call 'now glasses' instead of 'then glasses.' You can't truly understand why something was done or why a thing was the way it was if you cannot understand the values and mores that were observed at the time. Considering something in the past using today's societal values as the measuring tool will consistently lead you to incorrect conclusions.

"But Faulkner was an original. His writing style was unique and difficult to penetrate. You have to really get into Faulkner to read him in the way he wants you to. It's kind of like watching a movie at twice its normal speed. If you blink, you miss something, and while you're trying to make sense of what one character is saying, another character suddenly appears and affects the flow of the narrative.

"But if you really want to understand what Faulkner wrote, you have to understand Faulkner himself. You said earlier that his life was not difficult to understand, but I think you're just looking at the facts biographers have listed. Faulkner was, in essence, every bit as deep as his writing, and, in fact, he *is* his writing. He is instructing us in human nature—the human condition, if you will—and a goodly portion of that instruction comes from inside himself: his fears, needs, observations, assessments, and such.

"But remember that writers do not exist in a vacuum. For writers to be successful, there must be readers who want to read what is written. For example, if I were to write a book about Faulkner this year, do you suppose it would make the *New York Times* bestseller list?"

He waits while she swallows some banana from the fruit salad he has prepared.

"Would it be a good read?" she asks.

"Well, for the sake of the argument, let's say it would be a good read. No big words and no 'out there' philosophical concepts to wrestle with. Yes—a good, solid, entertaining book."

"So, why wouldn't it make the bestseller list?"

"I'll trade questions with you. If you weren't taking this course in Southern literature, would you be strolling through a bookstore looking for a book on Faulkner?"

"Oh…I see what you mean. No, I guess I wouldn't read Faulkner unless I had to. But wouldn't there be people in the literary world who would read the book?"

"You mean people like the editors at *The Southern Review* or *The Sewanee Review* or some other review or such?"

"Yes. Exactly. Wouldn't they be interested? And what about teachers and professors who teach Faulkner in their courses? I mean, I think my professor would probably read it. In fact, I know he would, because I would get you to autograph a copy and I'd give it to him!" She smiles at the thought of how much jealousy it would cause the other girls if she could establish a closer relationship with the soft-spoken, hunky professor who is old enough to be her father.

"There would be a few people who might buy the book if it were to ever be published, but therein lies the bane of every writer's life—getting published. You see, I have no standing to write a book about Faulkner. No PhD in literature, no previous publications, no standing in the literary community. I'm just someone who met Faulkner once and knew him well enough to predict that he would fall off a horse and it would kill him.

"Whoa!" She catches herself. "No pun intended," she says but giggles anyway. "You met Faulkner? I mean you actual-ly *met* him? Did you speak with him, or was it just like, you know, shaking hands?" She is excited because she is now seeing an "A" not just on the paper, but in the course. "Where? When? How?"

He is amused at her excitement. "Yes, I met Faulkner right here in Virginia, in—let's see, what was the year? Oh, how strange! It was 1960—the month before we elected our first Catholic president. Faulkner and I spent a good hour or so chatting. My Uncle Arch—your great-great-uncle—also knew him in Mississippi, and they kept up correspondence for a while. It's something we can talk about, but here's my quick take on Faulkner, and most other writers, for that matter. You can learn a lot from reading what they write, but you'll learn a lot more if you explore the writers themselves as you read. They tell beginning writers to 'write what you know,' which also means 'write what you feel.' So, by delving deeply into the authors' lives, you'll understand more, learn more, and appreciate the effort it took to write the story more.

"And the thing with Faulkner is—he can tell you a great deal about your cultural heritage and the Southerner's supposed longing for a different time. That's the thing about us true Southerners. In the back of our minds is this longing for another time—or at least so it sometimes seems. But Faulkner—while he longed to have been part of the antebellum South, and eventually in his own life achieved perhaps a dram of his longing—knew that the true South wasn't really a place of cavaliers or ladies in bright-colored crinoline hoop skirts living in big houses. That is not to say there weren't some big houses with ladies who occasionally wore hoops under their crinoline dresses, but that wasn't the true South. Less than 6 percent of the population of the South fit into the 'planter class' that has been immortalized in tales told of 'The Cause.' The other 94 percent were people working from day to day, year to year—just like everywhere else in the country. Small farmers, teachers, day laborers, storekeepers, and such. All and every trying to secure a better life for themselves, their families, and their progeny. Yet there was something—some hard-to-grasp ideal—that made them Southerners. And this, young lady, is what you're searching for. You'll find it eventually, but you may never be able to explain it. But if you can—if you can express it in words—you'll become a celebrated person."

"Umm..." Young Shelby struggles with the thought. "But I'm just a junior in college; isn't that something for someone older? Maybe it's what my professor should be looking for."

Shelby sips at his now lukewarm coffee, rises from his chair, and reaches for the coffeepot. "We need hot coffee in the mornings. Cold coffee is for the afternoon when the humidity and heat force you up into the shade of the veranda and the downdraft of a ceiling fan." Satisfied the pot has kept the coffee at the right temperature, he returns to the table.

"I suspect that is exactly what your heartthrob of a professor is looking for—and so is every other writer who affects himself a Southern author. It's what you have to look for and try to explain. Often, the best we are able to do is tell stories that we believe give some kind of substance to the otherwise amorphous ideal. It's like capturing universal truths in myth. It's hard, but it can be done. Are you up to trying?"

Young Shelby is still blushing as she considers his question. She had not meant to convey her secret crush on the professor—certainly not to her great-grandfather.

He decides not to wait for his question to be answered, for he is sure that she is, indeed, up to the challenge. Talking about such matters with her will give him reason for more meaningful conversation with at least one of his great-grandchildren, and perhaps draw them closer, but more importantly, it will ground another generation in the oral traditions of the family and their region.

"I'll send a note to the house in New Orleans and have them send my journal for 1960 up here, and I think your great-uncle actually had his daddy's journals and the letters from Faulkner digitized, so maybe we can just find them online or someone can send them to us on the computer. I think you'll find all these things illuminating."

"You keep a journal?" The blue eyes widen in disbelief.

"Of course. Don't you? Or do you call it a diary? You know, for the longest time women kept diaries and men kept journals. That is, unless of course, the woman was a writer, and then she called her diary a journal. Like Agatha Christie, perhaps; she kept journals. Anyway, maybe today you're all too busy, but people of my generation kept journals, and what with dementia and Alzheimer's and just plain forgetfulness, those journals can be a real boon to families. So, the answer is—yes, I keep fairly detailed journals of events that happen and how they affect me. I think you'll find my account of my morning with Faulkner an interesting read because I also record my impressions and predictions.

"So, how shall we do this? When's the paper due, and where will we work on it?"

Young Shelby tries to comprehend what is happening. She feels as if she is caught up in a Faulkner-written exposition, and the one that comes first to her mind is the opening description of the French general in *A Fable*, which she has just struggled to read. She is unsure of how to process the information, but she tries. "Well! You make it sound like Faulkner has challenged me to a duel. Me against Faulkner, with you as my second." She affects a long sigh but replaces it with a look of determination every bit as purposeful as

Scarlett's after Rhett has walked out on her. "Tomorrow is another day" and all.

"I suppose, being a Devereux, I'll have to accept. This is usually the quietest part of the day, but this has been one hell of a breakfast."

Shelby lets the descriptive expletive slide, but remembers that his Aunt Julia would have shaken a spatula at someone.

"So," young Shelby continues, "I think I would like to have breakfast like this, just the two of us. I've already learned more about Southern literature this morning than in the first two weeks of the course. And aren't duels always fought in the early morning?"

"Yes, I like that." Shelby is impressed. She really is bright and charming. "Yes, you and I at breakfast—and don't forget Faulkner."

"Oh, no! We can't forget him, for he'll be here every day, won't he? And we'll title the paper 'Breakfast with Faulkner.'"

ABOUT THE AUTHOR

TONY JORDAN GREW UP ON the Gulf Coast and graduated with honors from The University of the South in Sewanee, Tennessee. He served as a rescue helicopter pilot in Southeast Asia and later as an instructor, test pilot, and squadron commander in the US Air Force. He became a clandestine operations officer with the Central Intelligence Agency in 1979, where he earned many of that agency's highest awards during a twenty-six-plus-year career. After serving many overseas undercover tours as a clandestine operative and holding five senior leadership positions with the CIA at Langley, he retired, accepting a senior executive position with a major Boston-based research and technology company.

He now writes novels and short stories in the tower office of his cottage on Spy Hill Farm, in the foothills of the Crab Orchard Mountains of Tennessee, where he is ably supported and appropriately encouraged, when needed, by his wife, Anne, and his BFF, Tailwagger Jack.

If you enjoyed this book, please consider posting a review. Reviews on Amazon and Goodreads are gratefully appreciated. Independent authors depend on word-of-mouth recommendations and positive exposure through sites like these, so anything you can do to help publicize this and other books will help tremendously. Thank you.